D1405398

Elegies for Uncanny Girls

break away books

MICHAEL MARTONE

INDIANA UNIVERSITY PRESS

Bloomington & Indianapolis

Elegies for Uncanny Girls

JENNIFER COLVILLE

This book is a publication of

INDIANA UNIVERSITY PRESS
Office of Scholarly Publishing
Herman B Wells Library 350
1320 East 10th Street
Bloomington, Indiana 47405 USA

iupress.indiana.edu

The paper used in this publication
meets the minimum requirements of
the American National Standard for
Information Sciences – Permanence of
Paper for Printed Library Materials,
ANSI Z39.48–1992.

*Manufactured in the
United States of America*

*Cataloging information is available
from the Library of Congress*

ISBN 978-0-253-0249-9 (paperback)
ISBN 978-0-253-02436-7 (ebook)

1 2 3 4 5   22 21 20 19 18 17

Contents

Acknowledgments

I'd like to give special thanks to Robert and Susan Colville, my first teachers; to Chris and Katy Colville for pushing me in new ways; to my wonderful mentor Melanie Rae Thon—and longtime supporters Michael Martone and Karen Brennan. Thanks to Christine Wald-Hopkins, Gary Libman, Ann Kiley, Meg Files, George Saunders, Ann and Peter Pufall, and Lisa Roberts for encouragement and support. Thanks to my kick-ass workshop mates at Syracuse and Utah (you know who you are). To childhood collaborators and conspirators Robin Breault and Amanda Hunter Johnson, and to Sarah Bull Wald-Hopkins and Amy Buss. Thanks to Sarah Jacobi for taking a chance on these girls, and Betsy Schneider for the use of "Red Wax Lips." Thanks to my brilliant readers Susan Goslee and Bethany Shultz Hearst; to Peter and Frieda who remind me to dance. And thanks to Miles, for everything.

Elegies for Uncanny Girls

Other Mothers

I bump into the woman as I'm trying to maneuver my stroller out of the way of a man in a suit.

"Sorry," I say, turning around.

She laughs and lifts up her hands, and I catch sight of fine red seams at her wrist creases, seams that glisten and yawn as her hands tip backward, open to the bone so her hands topple like two people falling in unison over two peaks and finally hang, floppy but suspended behind the upheld stumps.

I'm stuck staring at the flesh inside the stumps. It's quivering, like the bunched-up petals of a peony, shaking on a wet bush. The bone is a piece of polished ivory set among jewels.

Wow, I think, is she truly avant-garde?

There are others who are like her at this café. Janet the barista, an artist who sometimes attaches labia made of bubblegum to her bare arms and face, à la the feminist artist Hannah Wilke; Jessie the cashier, whose earlobes have been stretched so far that for work the manager makes him tuck them over the tops of his ears as if they're locks of hair. There are the street kids outside. All blond dreadlocks and metal faces, and the often amputated bodies of the homeless, shifting and shuffling, toting their sleeping bags around like cocoons.

This woman fits in. Though, I'll admit I'm not sleeping well. It seems logical that my dreams, interrupted at night, have begun making daylight appearances.

Blood rushes to my cheeks. An erection of the face Freud called this, ever so helpfully.

"These coffee shops aren't built for strollers," the woman says. In the blink of an eye she's flipped her hands back up to her wrists, caught them on the stumps like that game in which a ball on a string is swung into its cup.

I'm confused.

But at least my baby is asleep.

I push my stroller up to the bar, where Janet is holding out my Americano. The café is full of the usual slumpy intellectuals, telecommuters, students, and hesitant light. I sit at a long table and when the woman is done ordering she comes and sits down at the far end, ensconcing herself between two piles of books. She smiles and nods again, opens up a computer, and begins to type. The seams at her wrists are barely visible now, slim, red, and glistening.

I pull out my notebook and try to get back to my list of things-to-do-to-get-my-professional-life-in-order-so-I-can-go-back-to-work-once-baby-is-in-daycare, but so far I only have this title. I look back at the woman. Though I'm generally pretty interior, I suddenly want to tell her about my life. Perhaps as an explanation for bumping into her? Perhaps because my weirdness won't seem so weird in the company of hers? Specifically, I want to tell her that it's been six months since the birth and I'm still afraid my baby will stop breathing.

I lie awake at night and the protocol from the class I took on infant CPR rolls through my head. The pumping of the rubber baby chest with two fingers, the horrible hollow collapse. I think, what if I should be doing this for my baby right now? I sneak to her crib and hold my finger under her nose to see if I can feel the push of air, but her nostrils are merely decorative! The whorl on the door of a seashell, two holes in a button. I lean further over her crib, try to *hear* the whisper of her breath or *see* the rise and fall of her chest. If I can't detect either I brush her cheek with the tip of my finger, or jostle her lightly, and then I run and leap under the covers before she calls out for me. I hide there sometimes while she cries.

I want this woman to say, "It will get better." I want this woman to be grand and all knowing, elevated like a therapist, or a scholar of female experience but not necessarily to have had any experience of her own. I imagine she'll squint her eyes at something in the air, an abstraction too fine and filmy for anyone else to see. She'll say, "Women are like Isis and Osiris, dismembered and resurrected. You have to celebrate your mutability, your disorientation of mind and body—have you read Cixous, or Kristeva?" And I will say, "Yes! But can you please explain them to me?"

I look at the woman. She's wearing vivid red lipstick, and has a scarf tied around her neck in a way that I imagine is very French.

And then she turns to me.

"How old is your baby?" she asks.

"Six months."

I wait for her to break into profundity.

After a long pause in which I probably look disappointed by the commonness of her question, yet can't think of anything interesting to say, she asks, "Are you wondering about my wrists?"

I shake my head and she holds one up.

"The hands won't fall off. But the split does make it harder to hold things." She extends her arm across the table, holding her wrist out for me to touch.

"They're hooked on here," she says, pointing to the space next to her wristbone. "This skin is thicker here. It's like a mitten clip."

I run my finger over the hinge, thick as cartilage, a small sturdy bridge of flesh.

When they pulled my baby out with the forceps she was gray and rubbery, and when they laid her down on my chest, only one of her eyes was open, the other swollen shut. Her mouth moved over my nipple, open, close, open, close, nuzzling, testing, trying and failing to make the proper latch.

The woman looks at me kindly, in a way that makes me want to check my blouse for splotches of food. She says, "Are you new to the city?"

"I've been here one year," I say.

"Well that explains it."

"What?"

"I mean, don't worry if you don't exactly feel grounded yet."

And I want to say, "Are you kidding me? This city is full of romantics! Look at all these millions of people crammed on this tiny piece of land with all its fault lines. Any day now we could fall into the ocean, but what's a little risk of dying when your art, or science, is going to save the world, when you're a self-important little person, with your big world inside your head. Can't you just see everyone's interior monologues bobbing along like cartoon bubbles, sucking up all the air?"

But I just stare at her, and she clears her throat and goes back to work.

I imagine it's good I didn't say this, because truthfully, when we arrived in San Francisco from Ohio we were these people. I'd just finished my PhD, I was ready to lecture at the university, to plunge into my writing career. And my husband Daniel, well, he certainly still *is* one of these people. He's off right now with his colleagues consulting and interacting, stimulating his brain. He's studying genes and growing cell lines, which are his babies outside of marriage. Often in the middle of the night he has to go in to the lab to check on their progress. He wonders, are they warm enough, are they being jiggled properly by the centrifuge?

"Have you made many friends?" the woman suddenly asks.

"Oh, the baristas," I say, and she laughs. And I laugh too, even though I didn't mean it as a joke.

"You haven't met other mothers?" the woman continues, a little sheepishly.

And I would suddenly like to go back to my list, because the answer is, "How can I avoid them?"

They are everywhere in this city.

Even now they are circling the café with their small and large strollers, their babies concealed under jackets and in backpacks, rounding corners and emerging onto the sidewalks of my neighborhood where I go to walk off the scary baby thoughts.

There I'd be, pushing my baby down the street, free for a moment among the yellow-green bay leaves, the flower boxes dripping with fuchsia, when another mother would barrel toward me with a baby strapped tight to her belly in a carrier like a huge bandage with no breathing hole.

Or, a baby facing out in a front pack would approach like a prisoner strapped to the front of a ship, its head bobbing forward and back. Its brain, I imagined, sloshing dangerously against its skull.

Or, a woman might walk by with a carriage, and I'd have to avoid eye contact, so as not to be drawn into a conversation only to find a baby wearing a neck brace—for this happened once. The woman looked away for one second and the baby fell off the bed.

And then there's the issue of mixing things up. Creating composites or superimposing, so that a baby from a distance might appear to have a black eye, or look small and sick like the preemie used to frighten young mothers out of bad behavior, hanging in my OB's waiting room.

But I don't say this.

I watch her carefully because now she's lifting her arm, pushing her chair out, and motioning to the end of the table toward the handles of a small umbrella stroller, handles which, before now, have been concealed by her books.

"I don't think you noticed," she says. And as she bends toward the stroller I gather my jacket, my notepad. I start to plan my escape. She sits quickly back up, and I use all the energy of my dread to fake delight and exclaim, "You have a baby too!"

But the woman has left her baby in the stroller. I settle back down in the chair and watch as she starts tapping her fingers nervously on the café table.

Tapping, and tapping, and staring off into space.

And I see that her eyes are bulging, as if tiny, nearly invisible words in Helvetica are moving across the white spaces—slipping behind the irises as if across a computer screen. I see that she has an interior monologue of the worried sort too.

Her face hangs in that blank look I feel on myself when Daniel knocks on my head and asks, "Is there anyone home?"

"Home?" I asked him the last time he did this. "I'm always at home. Why do you think my brain needs to be somewhere else?"

"You want to make me feel guilty?" he asked.

And I said, "Yes, I do."

I've tried to explain to him about the thoughts and images. I've tried to explain that I'm afraid I'm not a good influence, that when I gaze at our baby I see the beginning of my own furrow appear on her forehead, as if the pressure of my gaze has imprinted it there.

I've even suggested I work at the café so we have enough money to start daycare. But he reminded me about my PhD, and how I hated working in cafés, and he is right about the working in cafés part. He tickled me and said, "It's only six more months before you can go back to teaching."

Six more months.

I think that soon I'll have to tell him about the large bay windows that take up most of the wall in the two front rooms of our apartment above the Laundromat. The windows don't have screens, but I have to open them around three in the afternoon, when the October heat is too much, when the machines down below have been running all day, churning and thumping, thickening up the air.

I'll just tell him how it started with a simple image: me, tripping over a red toy truck, which evolved into my body, stretched out through the air as if diving for a football, except the football was the baby, knocked from my arms and sailing out through the window in slo-mo as I stumble to the sill and look down on a crowd of backs hovering in a circle—a useless human nest.

I'll tell him how I decided to stand closer and closer to the window with the baby, to challenge the image, to step right into my own shadow in order to make it go away.

This in fact worked for a while, until last week, when the scene changed into a fragment of an image, in which I leaned out the same window, over the same sidewalk, cradling my baby in both arms. And then I opened them.

I should probably tell him I've been avoiding the front rooms altogether now. That the baby and I play in the back room where there are bars on the windows. That even when we're safely out of the house, down on the sidewalk I feel as if I'm leaning out of a window, knees locked, thighs straining against the sill; that the effort to hold her, to keep her safe and to keep my balance, makes me nauseous, makes me feel as if San Francisco has shrunk to the size of a plank, and I'm standing on it, leaning, vertiginous, above the Pacific.

Back in the café a sadness is working its way through the woman's face, a blue half-shadow, a San Francisco, Humphrey Bogart shadow. The kind that cuts the face in half, confuses it like a shadow cast by the brim of a hat.

"It happened when I had my baby," she said. "That's when my wrists split."

And then it all makes sense. This woman isn't avant-garde. She isn't a French feminist. She's a mother.

"We had the babyproofers come in their white van," she said. "They installed foam padding on the tops of tables and bookshelves in case I drop her. They put locks on all the cabinets and got rid of our steak knives. They collected and disposed of anything small enough to be a choking hazard. Safety pins, buttons."

"Buttons?" I ask.

She looks at me suspiciously. "Haven't you read *The Educated Woman's Guide to Infants: Preventing Death, Dismemberment, and Delayed Development?*"

And I say, "I've just flipped through."

"Well, buttons are instruments of death," she says, eyeing the buttons running up and down my blouse. "They can lodge in your baby's throat and the Heimlich maneuver won't do a thing. The air from the pumps will just pass through the holes. You won't get enough pressure to pop it out."

She hunches toward her baby, her eyes bugging. And all of a sudden a small hand shoots up, wraps its fingers around a lock of her hair, and pulls. The hand rings her head gently—and as it bobs up and down she says, "I mean, I know it's all overboard. How do you have time to love your baby, if you're constantly preventing it from dying?"

And I say, "And if you don't prevent it from dying, how can you love it?"

And then I'm back in the delivery room, pushing.

The baby's heart is slowing down inside of me.

I'd been in the bed for two days when the nurses started to bend their heads together and murmur like pigeons. To glance quickly at the monitors and murmur some more. It was between the murmurs that I lost touch, floated up above myself with terror, and haven't yet been able to get fully back inside.

So the birth happened to me. I tried to be there but could only see it from a distance, through Daniel, the rotating doctors, midwives, nurses, and interns, the separate team of specialists hovering in the corner of the room, ready to whisk us away in the likely event that something went wrong. Even with all the drugs (and I had plenty), I couldn't escape this crowd of faces. Half of them quiet and concerned, half yelling or cheering me on as if I were a sporting event.

I couldn't get to that primal place my yoga teacher told me about, that place of grunting and moaning beyond caring what anybody thought. That place where I'd shed my vanity, where I imagined I'd turn animal, and porn star—turn into my mom and my sister and all the other mothers. I would turn common, and incredible.

Instead I asked for a C-section.

I said, "Wouldn't it be better?" And then . . .

"For shit's sake, her heart is slowing!"

And the doctor with the forceps propped over her shoulder said, "We don't do C-sections here. This is San Francisco."

Later my husband told me the forceps ripped me open like Jaws of Life tearing open a car. He said the young doctor pulled so hard on the forceps that she braced herself by placing one foot in front of the other and leaning back. Another doctor came in behind her, wrapped her arms around her waist, and pulled in this manner too.

And she was not breathing at first.

And she was not breathing.

Sometimes, even though I know my baby is healthy and growing—I'm still back in the delivery room. I think I see one of the faces, a doctor or nurse, displaced onto someone else's body on a crowded street, and I freeze. Freud would say deep down, I want to see these people, one of my strange witnesses. And I do wonder what would happen if we came face to face. Would they smile and say hello, feel happy to see me or the baby? Or would they be embarrassed for me or for themselves, would they avert their eyes? Most likely, I think, they wouldn't recognize me at all.

"Maybe we can go for a walk sometime," the woman says, as I put on my jacket and grab the handles of my stroller.

She scribbles her number down on a piece of paper, and holds it out. She says, "The worst of it is that I can't swim anymore." She holds up her hands again, now, like a supplicant, and a drip of watery pink blood falls on the table, before which I hesitate in my flight. I dig in my bag and offer her a baby wipe.

I've always been a swimmer—love that wonderful feeling of being underwater in a crystal womb you can look up through and see out of, see the world all bent, and different (I felt) from the way anyone else saw it. When I was younger I could swim entire laps underwater—push off from the wall, arms in front of me, pull the water toward my chest, kick, dart my arms up again, pull the water, cup it like a heart.

And as I remember this I realize I'm in front of the woman's baby looking down into the stroller.

It isn't wearing a neck brace.

She has no bruises. No safety helmet. She doesn't even have those blind soothsayer eyes that my baby has. That way of looking that sees everything and nothing—all my faults—and in an instant forgets, moves on to a fascinating piece of fuzz. Her cheeks are fat, nearly incandescent. She's a full year old, I'd guess.

She's smiling, holding her arms up and jerking them arrhythmically, as if jamming out to Stravinsky's *Rite of Spring*.

I turn back to the woman and say, "I like your wrists. I think they're cool. I mean, they could be like a statement if you want to keep them."

And before I go, I feel a pull and turn to see the baby is still really watching me. She latches onto my gaze and holds it in a challenge. She furrows her brow and throws her arms into the air, exploding her hands like stars. She jerks them back down and covers her eyes.

"It's her best trick," the woman says, and we smile at the baby's amazingly fat legs, for her disappearance has, of course, made her more visible.

"Ahh, ahh, ahh," the baby demands.

I say, "Whoa, girl, you've got skills," and then her laughter peals upward, buoyant and spreading. It's let loose like bunches of balloons, like all the babies who will grow into children, and then become teenagers despite their crazy mothers. It's let loose like all the babies who will learn to float free of their mothers, who will grow, however fitfully, into adults.

Costume

My brother is squeezable. I like to squeeze his head and rest my fingers on the soft spot at the top where the bones stay open, waiting for smartness to enter. I fit two fingers in this spot and rub in slow circles.

Today my brother is dressed as a pink bunny rabbit and I am a witch. My mother designed his costume because he's still too small to imagine for himself. He's at the stage where he hops around in his plastic underpants and eats the dog food. He lives in a round leaky world, with a round face and cheeks that are just waiting to be pinched, so he can have a pink face to poke out of his pink costume, with the satin hood that fits over his head like a ballet slipper, and the ears my mom spent hours on—carefully stuffing with pipe cleaners and pieces of cardboard.

"He's perfect," my grandmother says as she greets us at her front door on Halloween night. She carries him into the living room, props him up in the middle of the couch for all to admire.

"Oh, oh, oh," say my aunts of the long flowing hair: Delia the difficult, Annie who is worrisome, Sandra the serious and responsible. They gather around him and he sits there smiling and interpreting every word as a sign of love, every sound and smell as the goodwill of the universe.

"Yes," says my mom. He's her very own special creation.

I slide along the living room wall of my grandparents' house in my crooked glasses. I slide and creep. I've used masking tape to attach plastic eyelashes to my eyelids, to make my eyes appear more mysterious. My glasses have no lenses—all the better to see him with. I've made my costume myself, out of my mom's short silky green negligee, a witch hat, and fifteen Mardi Gras necklaces looped around my waist, neck, and arms for casting spells. I can see the future with my glasses, and in it I'll be good.

* * *

When it's time to take our Halloween picture the family assembles in the living room. I lift my brother off the couch and prop him up in front of me, against the coffee table. He lets me do what I want with him. Hold him up by his armpits, dangle him upside down over the edge of my parents' bed. I tell him in the bathtub not to feel bad about the weird thing between his legs: all boys have it and it's called a penis.

Now Grandma is yelling for someone to get Great-Grandma Mary who's losing her memory of us. She thinks the camera's flash will fix us, bright and smiling, in her mind. But Great-Grandma Mary is half-blind. She has to be fetched from the kitchen and wheeled up in her chair very, very close, and when she's finally in place and my aunts and uncles have gathered to see, Great-Grandma Mary leans across the coffee table and says, "Oh, what a beautiful geranium!"

"No!" my grandmother yells.

I settle my hands on my brother's head as my aunt Delia and my mom explain to Great-Grandma Mary what she's supposed to see. "The children! They're wearing costumes!"

But I like her originality.

I blur my eyes behind invisible lenses. I pat my brother's stomach, hug him, whisper "Shhh," and when he giggles and says "Shhh" back, I roll his satin bunny ears, very gently, bending the pipe cleaners and crunching the cardboard my mother spent such a long time on into two small handles.

Great-Grandma Mary leans closer, her eyes swimming behind glasses as thick as crystal balls. My father, who takes me out to shoot hoops, who treats me like a boy but will soon discover I'm not; Delia, who asked of my costume, "Whose idea was that?"; and my uncle, with the frightening voice, who yells, "My, what beautiful eyelashes you have!" all lean forward. They press in on us with their decisions about who is the best looking, who is too much of an individual, who is a little bit strange.

I smile, squint, blur my eyes and turn my family into shadows. But I can still feel them, filling us up with their different ideas, fastening us in place. My grandpa, steady with the camera, counts, "One, two," but before he can snap the shot, Great-Grandma Mary, whose voice is like water, says, "I see now. A pink bear, and a clever little witch," and my mother, much louder since she's begun taking art classes, declares, "No, he's a rabbit!"

I feel her love shoot an arrow straight at his costume. She spent one week with directions of feathery brown paper like maps, and tiny needles held between her teeth.

"I love the little babies," she likes to say. It's the little ones, she tells me, who need the extra attention, the extra patting and pinching; it's the little ones, I think, who don't ask questions, or want to do things their own way.

Grandpa aims the camera, centers us, and resumes: "One, two…" I look inside my great-grandmother's glasses, a space where people can change shape, fade, or completely disappear. I pull up, as tight as I can, on my brother's handles. The flash explodes into blinding light and then recedes into silver around the edges of everything. Globs of red and yellow move across the family's faces. Their hands rise to their throats. Their eyes pop. I let go of my brother's handles, and the room exhales. There is one tiny moment before he screams.

"Meredith!" my mom yells. "You were choking him." Her eyes and hair are loose. She runs toward me, pulls me by the upper part of the arm, the root. She pulls me down the hall and sits me down on a bed that used to belong to my father.

Now I have her full attention. I see I look strange to her in her silky nightie, slippery, like a piece of unstitchable satin. I wonder if it's the costume that makes me bad. I test it by running my fingers along my beads—I try to summon back their power. I smooth the folds of the negligee along my legs.

"Look at me!" my mother yells again, grabbing both of my arms, so I know she could shake me if she wanted.

"Why do you do things like that?" She reminds me that my brother is smaller than I am. That he needs to be protected.

I ask, "Do you like my costume?"

She takes a deep breath. Like me, she has a hard time not telling her truth.

She says, "It's very interesting." She says "interesting" the way she says it about the kids down the street who are allowed to run loose in their underwear, or about my outfits when my father dresses me. I start to feel crumbly inside, like we're separating, just slightly, like we're two of her skin-colored costume patterns slowly peeling apart. She hugs me and says, "I know you made it, sweetheart, it's nice, it's very, very. . ." She's running her hands over my beads, as if trying to feel their magic.

Center

Susan only half believes she's visiting the home of her newly married brother. She has a queasy, unreal feeling left over from the plane ride: New York to Los Angeles—nonstop, a feeling of distances covered too quickly. On the plane she'd studied the back of the inflight magazine—the states mapped out like different regions of the brain, the flight trajectories swooping and swirling electric pulses. She'd been surprised at the number of connections leading to and away from her childhood home in Cedar Rapids.

It didn't help Susan's sense of reality that the wedding, in her experience, was still just an image on the invite. The card had shown black-and-white photos of her brother and his fiancée making faces and kissing. She'd found the display of beauty and quirkiness annoying. And her annoyance made her feel like the "bitter older sister," so she'd taken the invite off of the refrigerator where she'd placed it as a reminder. She'd then lost the invitation, actually. She'd somehow managed to schedule an important part of her doctoral exams on the same day as the wedding.

Yet Susan now stands at her brother's front door, in a pocket of shade amid the bright LA sunlight, on a porch with a swing and other convincing realistic details like half-dead pansies in terra cotta pots. The door is cracked, and her brother Alex is rummaging around the car for the house keys he's dropped between the seats. Susan pushes the door open. She could call out to her brother, say, "Hey, it's open," but she'd rather be a spy. She'd rather check things out, make them her own.

It happens right away:

Inside the front room is a familiar slanted block of sun across a shaggy carpet, and pothos, hanging plants with their tropical twining leaves, like living wigs of long green hair. Here are the nubby cinder block walls. Although one is now painted a yellow ocher and seems to vibrate as if pregnant or alive. Susan is thirty-five, four years older than her brother, and she thinks, no, this is not his house, it's hers, the one she inhabited for that brief time without him, when she was the center of the universe.

Bubbles of romantically edited memory form:

She sits on the carpet inside the patch of sunlight and is spotlit underwater. Dust motes float like sea monkeys in the beam and the carpet is a jumble of aqueous worms.

But Alex, who has graciously picked her up at the airport, who is disconcertingly excited to see her, comes bounding through the door. "Oops," he says. He's a monstrously large child with orange leather bowling shoes and one sparkly earring. He shakes his keys in front of Susan's face. He skips to the kitchen, and destroys, as usual, Susan's romantic visions of herself—they rise, tremble, and pop.

The kitchen is very clearly not their old home. It's too California —the cabinets are white and sleek, not that old butterscotch brown with the faux-rustic hardware. There is a chrome dishwasher, refrigerator, and range. And Susan remembers that her brother's new wife Melinda is a "fancy cook person," as her mother called her. A gastronomist, with a blog and a personal consulting business. She is a yoga-doing, take-care-of-yourself-in-order-to-spread-good-vibes-across-the-universe person, Susan thinks. Enlightened bourgeoisie.

Little jars of herbs line the countertop. As if for more evidence her brother opens the refrigerator, which blooms into an exotic jungle of leafy greens, fruit as large as heads, blocks of cheese, and expensive blue and green glass bottles.

Susan thinks of her small Brooklyn apartment, meals of one precooked sausage, coffee, and gummy bears. She thinks about her brother's old refrigerator, full of beer and half-eaten bags of French fries—oh, how they bonded over their bad health habits.

Alex now sticks his hand into the green mass and pulls on something beige and full of twisted appendages, something that grows larger as it emerges from the leaves. "It's a root baby," he cries and drops it suddenly on the counter. He takes a few steps back and laughs, at first forced, then real.

Susan has her choices—she can laugh along with her brother and bond over the sudden weirdness. An ironically random message from the universe?

Instead she takes the laugh and tries to unravel it.

She thinks the laugh is partly for her sake, a way to say, "Don't worry, older sister, I haven't been domesticated either," and she doesn't like the pity.

She thinks the laugh might carry a tinge of self-congratulation—a satisfaction that his unfamiliarity with root vegetables is proof he's still antiestablishment, still a struggling artist, even if fully funded by his wife.

She thinks the laugh comes from a fear that they're no longer neck and neck, a fear that he's fallen behind. She's still out there in the real wilds—not those of a suburban refrigerator, but like Baudelaire or Basquiat (Alex's heroes), those of a real city.

But Alex doesn't seem to be thinking anything. He bounces around the kitchen, working a fancy espresso machine, and tells her about all of his projects: he wants to fill in the swimming pool with soil and grow a huge urban garden, because that would be so anti-LA; he'll sell his car if Melinda lets him and turn the garage into his studio. He'll get a bus pass and become the flâneur of public transit, "because how else do you see real people in LA?" He laughs at himself, and Susan hears that large portion of humility and grace, an excitement that stretches far back and bubbles up from their childhood, a time when having a new toy, something magnificent all to himself, meant he wanted to share it with her.

She sits on the carpet inside the square of sunlight beamed through the living room window. He buzzes at her edges, watches her carefully, and leaps into her beam of light. She plants her hand in the middle of his chest, and shoves him hard.

She moves to the kitchen table and wills herself into the tip of a crayon. She makes water with blue and yellow waves, but can see through the door that baby Alex has already forgotten he's been shoved. He's trying to take her sea monkeys and capture them in a glass jar. He dances and leaps in and out of the beam, and scatters the dust motes everywhere.

Susan draws a storm.

Alex swipes the glass through the air and covers it, quick, with the metal lid. She hates how her brother wants to see everything she sees, and then copies it. She knows their mother will always give him more encouragement for his efforts because he will always be younger, and, like the little engine that could, the one who is always trying to catch up.

Until now, that is.

Susan focuses. She tries to center herself in the present, at the kitchen table, while her brother flits around the kitchen offering "coffee, water, wine?" Her eyes land on a row of her brother's photographs hung along the yellow ocher wall.

They're images of cow eyeballs with the long nerve still attached. Her brother collected the eyeballs at butcher shops, placed them on copper emulsion plates, and let the images develop from the eyes' juices. *Eyes so potent that even though the nerves were severed they left an impression, leaked out rings of orange and green phosphorescence—left a chemical spill.*

They're fossil eyes, Susan thinks, poisonous and trapped in their old ways of seeing.

When she'd first seen them, she'd dismissed the photos for being weird for the sake of weirdness. But she'd seen them alongside some older images. The ones in which Alex had pierced his collarbones, draped a Superman cape from the piercings, and photographed himself looking like an ambivalent golden boy—the blood from the piercings still trickling down his chest. "Oh, the martyrdom of the white male," she'd teased him. He'd laughed a little and said something about being in art school and what was he supposed to do? He couldn't exactly make empowering art about his vagina.

But now by themselves the eye prints are different. Beautiful, actually, like flying over salt flats and marshes; the cornea is an island in a swirling salt sea.

Susan tries to remember the theory behind them. She drifts off when her brother explains his theories, which usually seem a painful reminder of how she once sounded, and maybe still sounds—strivingly pretentious in a way they both thought would impress their father. Their beloved father who was gentle and kind, but who spent a large portion of their childhood grading papers and sealed in a bubble of seriousness.

Looking at the eye prints she thinks she should say something, give a compliment. In fact, had she ever complimented Alex's work?

Alex comes to join Susan at the dining room table, proudly carrying a tiny cup of espresso on a saucer. As he sits down Susan notices a Native American dreamcatcher hung on the wall behind him, probably not authentic—the kind of white-person appropriation you can find at any gas station in the Southwest. She smiles wickedly and says, "That must be Melinda's."

Her brother turns his head to look at the dreamcatcher and then smiles back at her.

"You know Melinda's a little nervous around you," he says.

And Susan, caught off guard, doesn't believe it.

Susan is in no way better-looking than Melinda, nor is she in any measurable way more accomplished. Susan has lofty-sounding goals; she wants be a poet-scholar. She wants to travel and give readings, to finally find a volumizer that will allow her to flip off witty comments as she flips her wild mien of poetess hair. Susan wants to pass the theory phase of her orals, to fucking finally understand Derrida's semes, Freud's overdetermination. (She's nailed Barthes, however, and will probably end up reading about his starry open texts for comfort, after she obtains her PhD and is living in a homeless shelter.)

Melinda, on the other hand, has a job, a house, and her brother.

And speaking of the yogi, Melinda suddenly appears in the frame of the small arched door, slipping off her shoes, placing her yoga mat under a low bench. She deposits her keys with a jangle, as if to clear off Susan's bad energy, into a scalloped metal bowl.

Melinda, Susan thinks, has the power of those people who don't announce themselves, upon whom your gaze happens accidentally, so you're struck by their self-containment, by the way they don't need you to exist. Susan wonders where Melinda found her internal ruler because she doesn't seem to measure her actions against others. It's a ruler that's implanted in her spine—her posture is stick straight.

She moves toward Susan. She hugs her warmly, looks her in the eyes and, smiling, says, "I'm so happy you get to visit us. How long can you stay?" And as quickly as she asks this she separates and returns to her business about the house, as if Susan has created nary a ripple in the smooth surface of their lives.

"I'm just staying one night," Susan says, watching, wondering how her brother ended up with someone so weird, or, more accurately, so unlike either herself or her mother.

And her mother, Susan thinks, as she watches Melinda glide around the furniture, her mother has donated more than the kitchen table, where she sits at this very moment. The kitchen table with the familiar scratches. She hovers her hands over it now as if guiding a planchette along a Ouija board. Items like the old sewing machine, the rocking chair, items that would normally be donated to an oldest daughter, are emerging in the room like large rocks in the shallows. Her eyes bump up against them and they make jarring unattached thoughts.

Susan presses her hands firmly against the top of the table. She tries to center herself, to be centered like Melinda, but instead she remembers her hands running over her mother's stomach as it grew thicker and harder, became occupied with her brother. Her mother's radical change happened when she was four. It must have become clear then that her mother was a separate person, not Susan's constant background, her soft cushion with breasts. Her blanket, or bigger version that she could fit snugly inside.

Her mother is bursting. Susan puts her hand on her stomach. She feels the new hot of her skin and knows that ground shifts, that flesh splits—and although inside her mother's belly she knows that her brother is really only as big as her head, she understands volcanoes, and earthquakes, and that the earth is attached to a string, suspended and spinning.

Or, her mother is lying in bed, sweaty and a little sick, and Susan wants to help, but the mother is the unhelped helper. The primary source. She leaves the drinks Susan brings untouched on the nightstand.

Melinda opens the refrigerator. She takes out a blue bottle, a mango, and settles down between Susan and Alex at the kitchen table. Susan has to admit, she likes that Melinda doesn't try to serve them, doesn't offer anything from the refrigerator. Her mother did this compulsively, especially on Susan's visits home from college, and Susan thought it was a kind of apology for no longer being close, and that if it was an apology, it was also a way of staying separate, a way of maintaining her own bubble of domestic control.

Melinda, Alex, and Susan sit at the table, and the sun is hovering just above the sliding glass door, lighting up the chips and scratches on the table where they once sat as children over large bowls of cereal. And Susan can't control herself. She turns to Alex and says, "When you were born, I didn't want to share Mom."

Melinda looks up from her mango, but not suspiciously, like Alex. Just curious.

Alex laughs and says, "How do you even remember?" He says, "I think you're writing a story."

"No," says Susan. "That's why I was so mean to you."

But Alex rolls his eyes, and looks toward Melinda. He says, "You weren't that bad."

"But maybe that's why we're still so competitive," Susan says. "Don't you ever have that feeling, like we're stuck together on a teeter-totter? If one of us is sailing up, the other is watching—sinking from below."

"What?" asks Alex, shaking his head. "Are you saying this is why you missed the wedding?"

But Susan pushes aside his incredulity. His question too. She feels a memory coming on.

Susan remembers that once her brother came, she felt she had to move on, away from her mom, and that made her feel very small at first. Her hair looked so thin in the mirror in her mother's bathroom, a mirror the size of the huge landscape paintings at museums. Her mother had finally shown her the mirror when she lifted her onto the counter to tie large felt bows to the ends of her braids for a family picture. The bows immediately made the braids look as thin as toothpicks. Her mother chuckled at the disproportion—loved the awkwardness of her children, loved them most, Susan thought, when they didn't understand things, looked silly, or needed her help.

And of course, Susan didn't want to be a baby or a clown. She knew that although her mother said she could help with her new baby brother, it wouldn't be true. She suspected her mother and her brother would be one person until her brother was at least three, and by that time she'd be seven—practically an adult.

Susan remembers working hard on being independent, on strategies for making herself into her own landscape, house, or womb. She remembers her friend from down the street who played by putting dolls under her dress and tucking the dress into her underwear. But she didn't want to be only a mother—she wanted to be mothered, too. She wanted to be wrapped in layers and surrounded by something bigger and more beautiful than herself, but that she'd created.

She learns how to climb up into the cherry tree, lie in the crooks, and let her thoughts reach out like branches, and bud into capillaried walls.

Or, she brings flashlights under the covers when she's supposed to be sleeping and learns to read inside the stomach of her orange felt blanket. Each word is a pulse. If she doesn't know it, she makes it up, quickly, so as not to skip a beat.

Melinda floats through her routine like a planet on a mobile over a crib. Susan wonders if the brother is rendered docile by Melinda's steady orbit, so different from their mother's—she always hurried and bumped into furniture, sometimes injured herself trying to keep the house clean. Susan sips her coffee.

She's pissed that her brother implied she was writing a story. "So what if I'm writing a story?" she says aloud. "According to Zola a story is a scientific experiment, it's a hypothesis—it tests an idea."

"Whatever," Alex says, and then, "I think you should test a story through multiple points of view."

"Like yours?" Susan asks.

"Yes," says Alex, "and Mom's."

"Oh, I think I know Mom's point of view," Susan says.

But then she immediately realizes that this is the heart of the problem: of course she doesn't.

Beside the dreamcatcher Melinda has hung a painting of a newborn baby. Susan finds the picture startling, and the newborn ugly and unhappy-looking, with his eyes squeezed shut, a hospital bracelet cinched around his wrist, and little fists like prunes held up to his face. The paint around him is smeared, as if he's emerging from dust, or exhaust. She wonders how Melinda doesn't see the pained expression on his face. At the same time, she admires Melinda's ability to know her wish and to hang it in the center of the wall.

Susan stares at the painting and then back at Alex. She points to it and raises her eyebrows as if to say, What does this mean?

Alex stares back at her. "Melinda put that up because she's friends with the artist." Susan narrows her gaze and looks at him.

"Oh, and I think it's very beautiful, don't you?" Melinda calls out from the kitchen.

Susan smiles at her brother, who has dodged her question: Does Melinda want a baby?

She knows he's scared. For the moment, she's won.

The sun is now burning a bright seam along the metal rim of the sliding glass door. It casts a reflective light across surfaces, burns them out. Susan walks into the living room and runs her hands along the soft nubby walls. She likes the eclectic nondecorating decorating style. It seems familiar, similar to her own attempts to be both domestic and not. The room, though, is definitely tinged with Melinda. On the bookshelves are funny Dadaist knickknacks like a log wearing a sweater, mixed with what are probably expensive crystal wedding gifts from the wedding she didn't attend. There are old gas station signs and a couple of large salty-looking crystals. And it all begins to blur. It's as if all the objects are hanging together on one web, on Melinda's dreamcatcher. At least from the outside their lives are already like one of those double-image pictures that change depending on your angle of vision; their lives seem inexplicably intertwined. And Susan begins to give in, to let go of her resistance. She's going to be an aunt. Probably. Isn't it just like a bitter older sister to try to unravel a brother's happiness? To criticize and poke holes? Shouldn't she hope that somewhere in this vivid, clunky web, there will be a space for her?

The irony is that Susan didn't, at first, care to be loved by Alex, nor did she notice his love, except as an annoyance, or a constant background, like a wall painted yellow that bleached to electric white during adolescence but would blossom brightly on their returns from college, and then bleach back out again, after a couple of days, to an annoying hum. From a certain angle, her brother's love was great and undeniable, as obvious as an amaryllis bloom. But she's been having to read Plato and Lacan, and is half convinced that Alex's love came mostly because she was so busy without him. She half believes that all love comes from a desire to fill a perceived lack in oneself, a something missing that her brother, for instance, thought she had.

Another irony is that even though she probably seemed full to Alex she was in fact overcompensating for the lack she felt in relation to her mother. She was always busy making things for the mother, trying to show her she was separate and fully grown. She had factories—salt-dough ornament factories, Shrinky Dink factories, painted egg factories, and origami assembly plants. She wanted to be independent but also wanted her mother's approval. Here, at least her brother's love was useful; she let him be a helper, sometimes even a partner if he let her dress him as a girl.

Or, "let" isn't the right word. He liked to be dressed as a girl, especially when they organized shows for their mother, when they went into her makeup bag, sat before the big mirror, and unzipped the mother's secret factory of pink and coral lipsticks, silvery gray eye pencils, and blush in pots shaped like seashells.

Susan pushes a chair to the counter and tells Alex to climb up. They sit cross-legged with the cool Formica against their bare legs, tingling all over at the thrill of invading their mother's space. This time she's gentle. She tells her brother not to be afraid, because she isn't sure about how to apply the makeup. She tells him to stop moving, places one hand on his forehead, and presses the back of his head against the medicine cabinet. His eyes shiver, are separate little organisms, and he lets out an "ah" at the pressure of her hand, but Susan is transfixed by the tiny lungs of the iris, their feathery expand and contract, the mucous-tipped end of each tapered eyelash, all of them embedded in a perfect row. And she is equally entranced with her mother's tube of mascara, with unscrewing it, and the small pop of suction it makes when the brush comes out of the tube. As she brings the wand down to the base of the lashes Alex blinks, and the wand ricochets down his cheek. Susan says, "One more time," holding his head back, and "One more time," again, until her fingers are pitchy and his eyes are swirling black storms.

Susan picks up a glass prism, a knickknack off the coffee table, and sees her own eye enlarged, as opaque as a cow's. She feels a flood of affection for Alex—who stayed still for the torture. Did he stay still because she was finally looking at him with the interest she gave to her projects or books?

There were things that she hadn't seen about her brother.

"Your brother wanted to be like you," her mother liked to say. "And he had such a hard time with reading, you know. We had to get him tutors. He needed extra help."

Susan did remember Alex's trouble with *spoken* words, how they came like twitches, how they came like small explosions from caps— the plastic rings filled with powder that he would take outside and hit for hours with rocks.

But she also remembers how many of her brother's tics were also, annoyingly, hers. There was the compulsive eye twitch she developed in junior high. Her brother developed a stronger case of it after she'd gotten over hers, and she would cry "Stop!" when she saw him, sure that it was contagious and that she would be reinfected. And she was hypersensitive to his chewing, and to the strange way he had of breathing and talking through his extra-large retainer, like a minia- ture drooling Darth Vader. Her father, she remembered, had laughed when Alex learned to take out the retainer and set it next to her dinner plate, dripping with saliva.

And yes, she'd been mean to him. Because all their faults seemed horribly interconnected, as if he were her dark shadow, or ghost in the closet. Their quirks and compulsions repeated themselves on each other's bodies in only slightly different ways.

And Susan suddenly loses her balance on the high countertop, and Alex rolls away from the medicine cabinet, is tipping, falling over the edge, and here comes her terror, and the pang; there is her bruised love for her brother, rising up in the panic. She wonders if, now, she can come out of memory, ready to love her brother in the present, but her brother is screaming because he's hit his head on the toilet and is stuck in the garbage can, and their mother is rushing into the bathroom and pulling him out in one mighty swoop, grabbing Susan at the top of her arm, the root, and pulling the two of them together. She's found the mascara wand—she holds it up and says, "You cannot use this on your brother. Look at him. Look. You've hurt his eyes." And Susan, who was hoping her mother would appreciate the subtlety with which she was going to apply the mascara, sees that Alex is really fine, feels her pride push up, and says, "I like him better as a girl." Her mother, shaking, says, "You're not the center of the universe." She says, "Someday he'll be bigger than you," and Susan feels the earth shifting, thinks of buildings falling down in slow-motion films. Somewhere, amid the rubble, her mother is saying, "Someday, much later, you'll want him as your friend, and he won't have forgiven you."

Susan is back in the living room. She could at least tell Alex that she likes his photographs. But their mother is there too. She's in the furniture, in the air between them, in a way that seems to push all other relationships out.

Susan asks instead, "So, how is the art going?"

And it's the wrong question.

Alex deflates and puffs up at the same time.

"Great. Great. Fine," he says. "This LA art scene, it's all about *who* you know." He leans back in his chair, props his feet up on the table to display his orange leather bowling shoes, and tries to look intense. Susan wants to ask him, But are you actually working? She wants to make a comment about the importance of daily hard work over being charming and making connections.

Instead she asks, "Did it ever bother you that Mom always thought you had to do the same things I did?"

"No," Alex says with a defensive tinge in his voice that makes Susan realize he has thought about it. "She encouraged us to do the art because she loved it, because she probably wanted to do it herself."

"Well, she should have been an artist, then, and left us alone."

"There's still time," Alex says, a little annoyed. "It's not like her life is over."

Susan thinks this might be true. Last summer, on a visit home, she'd come across one of her mother's creations in a consignment shop in Cedar Rapids. There were the painted paper birds, delicately stitched onto a wire frame made to look like a birdcage. The birds hovered outside the cage, in a variation on a theme—as if to say, "We're not trapped. It's our choice to belong to a home."

And then on this last visit, after Susan had been away for nearly two years, her mother had changed. She didn't rush so much—she actually sat still, and looked at Susan, as if ready to listen. At dinner, there was a new kind of smile on her father's face when he looked at her mother—and the wine bottle—when had they started drinking wine? In fact, her mother was wobbly when she leaned over, grabbed Susan's hand under the table, and said, "I try, but I never say the right things with you." Susan noticed that her eyes were shivering, like her brother's—there was that glossiness of tears forming, and that feathery expand and contract.

Susan had tried to hold on to this, even if, upon reflection, she could have used it much earlier on. That night in her old bedroom in Iowa, she'd opened the window to let in the air with its crush of cicada sound and humidity, its intense aliveness. And things her mother had said floated back to her. They hovered. Sharp and out of context.

She'd said:

I think you do things to prove to yourself that you can do them and not because you really want to.

Or,

Writers have to be really driven, and you're not like that. I don't think driven people are happy.

Or, when Susan was excited to go back to school again:

I suppose you need to do that. I just hope your brother doesn't think he has to do the same thing.

Back at the dining room table Alex has grown cocky. Susan can tell he's preparing to say something when he stands up from his chair—he says things in transit so people don't see them coming and so he can make a quick getaway.

"Who's to say Mom isn't an artist," he starts tentatively.

And then, bam, adds. . .

"We don't all need awards and degrees to make ourselves real."

"If you're a woman in a patriarchy," Susan says, "who needs to support herself, who doesn't have a nice sugar mama, actually, they help."

Bam.

"Well, if it's still such a patriarchy, why do I have a sugar mama?"

Bam, sort of. . . .

And then her brother is gone, out the sliding glass door. She can see him reach in his pocket for cigarettes, pretending everything is cool, as he does, or truly shaking it off and leaving Susan to wallow in her evil sisterhood.

Alone, Susan goes back to thinking about her mother, but also about how it would be too hard to be any mother. If she were her mother she might have done the same things. She might have told Alex that if his older sister had learned to read and speak quickly he could get tutors—he could learn fast too. Or that if his sister could draw and win art prizes, he could take lessons—he could win some too. And if his sister got a scholarship and went out of state for college he definitely *should* do that, even if he said no, slammed doors, and began sinking into a deep well of apathy and high school suspensions. Even if it meant that she, the mother, would have to fill out his college applications for him, and she and Susan would have to drive him halfway across the country, depressed and hungover, and deposit him on his campus of fairy tale turrets and creeping ivy, a campus he soon grew to love, a much more prestigious school than Susan went to, and that Susan was so jealous of.

Susan had filled out one out-of-state college application, fearfully, and covertly, and when she got accepted with a partial scholarship, her announcement was met with surprise and fear. Fear that there wouldn't be enough money? Fear that she wouldn't succeed?

But Susan has to admit, it was her mother, her mother who gave up school to marry her father, to raise Susan and her brother, who finally joined her side. It was her mother who fought for her, who finally got her beloved father to change his mind.

She knows her mother fought for her.

She was her mother's only child for four whole years.

Her mother had carried her in her belly for nine months.

At one point she'd been everything.

Now Susan wonders if her mother hadn't been able to look in the right way at her brother either. Her brother wasn't lacking just because he was younger or fundamentally agreeable, or because he wanted to be like Susan, like a girl. He wasn't lacking anything until first their mother and then Susan looked at it that way. Maybe her mother looked at Alex too much through the lens of the original sister, just as she seemed to look at Susan too much through the lens of herself, through the lens of what she had, or hadn't imagined she could do.

Now Susan is suddenly in motion, as if she's grabbed on to something hard and useful. The walls and furniture have started to solidify and become one place instead of two, and she gains enough leverage to get up and help Melinda who's been chopping, blending, and wrestling with the root baby in the kitchen.

Standing next to Melinda with her hands in the dishwater, she sees it, a tiny painting she did for the brother in college, a silly painting—a still life of a photo, the Man Ray eye, with teardrops attached to the ends of each eyelash in crystalline bits of glue. Why did she make a painting of a photograph? It was a pop art phase, she thinks, or maybe a comment on how we see the same things over and over, as if we have only one or two templates in the brain? Anyway, it wasn't very successful. The paint is flat in some places, muddy in others, yet her brother has found a place for it on his wall.

When Melinda, Alex, and Susan sit back down at the old kitchen table, Susan tries to be an adult. They're older now, and she should let go of her mother, who she can't truly understand, who is a different person now than she used to be. Alex has things that Susan doesn't. He's even moved ahead of her, or was always ahead of her in terms of generosity, and seeing outside of himself.

He's shaken his irritation off, or so it seems, and is offering her a glass of wine.

Susan notices that he has a hard wrinkle at the corner of his mouth. So does she, but his is bigger.

She knows she should tell him how much she likes his beautiful photographs, but instead she asks, "Do you remember when I tried to put mascara on you and you fell into the wastebasket?"

Melinda gasps and smiles, and Alex, lifted by her interest, meets Susan's eyes, says, "No. What happened?"

Susan exclaims with joy and terror, "I thought I permanently damaged you. Mom thought I had ruined your eyes!" and Alex looks a little worried about where the story is going, so Susan says, "But I obviously didn't."

She gestures to the walls of the house, to the photographs, and the clutter and Melinda. And her brother, who has been ready to be her friend since she walked in the front door, settles into his seat and says, "Tell me what happened." And Susan, aligning herself with Alex, begins.

Caroline

In the picnic area behind the swimming pool, shielded by a small pocket made by pomegranate trees, we folded paper into prisms and wrote names of boys under folds we colored like peacock feathers. To land a boy you picked a number and watched your friend's fingers open and shut the prism—nineteen, twenty times—felt your face flush as you leaned over and unfolded one of the petals. Your friend held your future in her hands and the boy you would ride into it, as if he were a chariot. We'd be asleep, like some of our mothers; or driving, with a whip.

But the revealed boy—even the one you secretly wanted—paled in comparison to the conjuring, the making of the prism, the secrecy, and the power of your friend's fingers, voice, breath. Inside our folds—under our arms and behind our knees—we also loved one another. Remember? The one who was you, but different. The one you were supposed to leave behind.

I loved Caroline. Caroline, because we didn't go to the same school and had to wait for each other, in stiff winter clothing, for summer when we could be mostly naked.

School was bad for many reasons, one of which was that I only had one pair of jeans with the right insignia embroidered into the small front pocket. That horse's head I imagined would make me run fast, or gallop along the beach like the girl with long flowing hair who wore these jeans in the commercial. Instead it put me in with two girls with similar jeans and through the long school months we walked in a defensive wall, arms linked against boys and their bad words—bitch, douche, snatch, slut—or against other girls and their lesser outfits.

During sixth grade our movements nearly stopped. We walked in our wall, or sat in a circle on the playground trading stickers. A yellow heart for a red balloon, a boring teddy bear for a fat rainbow attached to a cloud. I didn't dare trade for what I really wanted—the stickers from boutiques that Melissa Carlyle owned: the Mylar disco ball, the mood stickers filled with swirls of oil that seemed intricately connected to her royal essence.

And it was the year the school nurse marched into our classroom and sent the boys out into the hall. She was on a hunt for the bandit girl who was clogging the toilets with maxi pads. She held one up. Exhibit A. I was surprised to see that the pad looked harmless, like a small boat made of clouds. I imagined I'd put one between my legs and sail into a different, more dangerous land.

Summer was another land. Of public swimming pools, and vacations with Caroline's family to the beach in California. For four years we'd caravanned across two states, hot and sticky inside cars without air conditioning, surrounded by the smell of siblings, and car food—dank apples and raisins that stuck to our legs like large moles.

Among the welter we kept our status as rulers by reminding each other we owned the only two pairs of roller skates among five brothers and sisters—and we envisioned California, where we'd skate free along the sidewalks that wrapped around our campgrounds. Our background: a soft-rock album cover—a silhouetted palm tree and a fuzzy orange-and-yellow sunset. We'd be miniature roller-skating Amazons—our legs, strong from swim team, would glisten with coconut oil.

Of course our parents usually made us share our roller skates.

So for this we devised a plan.

We took off one skate each, tossed the other over our shoulder to a waiting brother or sister, and joined ourselves in motion by skating on our inside legs and holding each other's waists for balance. We had to force our legs in because they kept moving out, as if our combined body was doing the splits, and we had to keep our inside legs hitched up for one, two, four seconds until we fell into each other like heavy flamingos. We would skate and crash. Skate and crash. We made a pocket of stunted motion—until we sealed ourselves together by being stupid and the same.

And we were the same. The summer we were seven, we each lost a front tooth in the same week. Our swim team bathing suit was the same bright blue, so when we dove underwater our bodies blurred into identical rippled sea creatures. The woman who sold us ice cream said, "You must be sisters." And once, after a sleepover, Caroline's mother told us that we'd talked to each other while we slept. She'd heard our voices at three o'clock, but when she went to check on us our eyes were closed, our lips gently moving. We were talking in our dreams!

After this I was afraid to sleep over. Not that night, but the weekend before, I had a dream I didn't want Caroline's mother to hear.

I'd dreamed of weddings. Of everything so white, as if I'd been trapped by the tiny white dots of a TV screen, or buried in a hole in the snow. I was at my aunt's wedding, standing below a huge cake, when the cake fell over—the four-story cake that was the shape of a woman in a wedding dress. It hit the ground and exploded as if it had been shot. That's when Paul's face came to me, panting, as if he'd run miles to catch up. I woke up in the dark and said, "I'll marry your brother so we can be sisters." Caroline rolled over and mumbled, "I do."

The last summer we went to the beach was between sixth grade and junior high. It was the summer our mothers ganged up on us.

There was a plan afoot. We felt it! We were separately persuaded to leave our swim team suits at home—the one-piece racers that made our bodies safely one solid unit. Caroline's mom had bought her a green string bikini, and I was there the day she pulled it out of the shopping bag, slowly, like a slippery eel, and dangled it in front of Caroline's eyes.

I'd bargained for a fat bikini that fit tight across the top and flattened me out. Still, there was my stomach. Moony and separate. Loitering between the upper and lower parts—in dialogue with nothing.

This summer we wore our T-shirts until the last possible moment, until we saw the ocean.

Driving into the parking lot, everyone tried to see it first, but it wasn't like spotting the swimming pool as we approached in our carpool at home, it wasn't that single thing we could point to. It was a wide blue band that saw us. Had us surrounded. It made us scream as we ran down the beach, and finally pull off our shirts as if making a sacrifice. And then we ran faster. As the beach hit a steeper slope, as our feet began running without us. We sharpened ourselves into sleek spears of motion because our brothers were behind us, trying hard to catch up.

Although I didn't mind this year about Caroline's brother Paul.

We tried to play our tricks on Paul while he slept. Toothpaste mustache, painted toenails, or bicycle-pump-in-belly-button—a stunt that made a great farting noise. But Paul was older than my brother who slept through most things and, when he did wake up, was excited by the attention and ready to try the farting-belly-button trick on himself. Paul set traps at his door; tin cans that clattered over when we tried to sneak up on him. Paul would scream ferociously if he woke to find us near his bed. He had wild hair streaked by the sun, and he once told me I had beautiful arms.

I felt him running behind me, and I paused. I let him tag me on the back.

And that was when Caroline lost the top of her bikini.

She was ahead of me, so I didn't see it happen, but I imagine it like something from Ovid. The wave enfolding her like a hand of watery fingers, untying the bikini and tossing it gleefully, a flimsy piece of seaweed; a god's laughter booming up along the shore.

I remember how the beach looked junkier than usual, littered with wrappers and cigarette butts, and one slimy flesh-colored balloon. I remember the feeling as I stopped and didn't rush in that something had shifted. California, the beach, and nature had conspired with our mothers. The world was doubly exposed and slightly outside of us—no longer in alignment with our desires.

Caroline stood waist deep, in a pause between waves. She was a blank space, pulled out of motion and stuck. The wave must have hit her from behind because her hair was slicked forward in the style we called the sea creature for its resemblance to an octopus, attached to and sucking on a head.

Paul lifted his arm and pointed. He laughed in loud loose goose honks and I laughed too, for just a moment.

I laughed the way we did every summer, stopping on the boardwalk to point at the woman on a sign with breasts made of light—two red bulbs flashing on and off in the centers.

I laughed as Caroline threw down her hands to reveal two semibreasts, pink and puckered like baby mouths.

I laughed because although my bandage bikini flattened me out, underneath my breasts were growing like individual organisms in their own idiosyncratic ways.

I laughed because I felt the slap of the waves hit her frame, the punches of my own laughter, Caroline's blood burning up through my skin.

And I didn't help when Caroline launched toward Paul, took him underwater, and then rose, I hoped, like a new kind of creature born out of the sea. She ran up the beach, fast, her body blurred to a bright white streak. She ran to what looked like the edge of the world. The seam where the sky met the uneven line of sand.

I walked up the beach slowly, and lay down next to Caroline, but at a distance. She'd found her T-shirt and bunched it into accordion ridges across her chest.

"I'm sorry," I said.

She sat up and shrugged. "About what?"

I didn't say anything.

After a while she mumbled, "We could bury them," and I felt relieved, remembering the game in which we buried our brother and sister in the sand and then surprised them by saying, "We now pronounce you man and wife." She reached over, squeezed my arm too tightly, and used it as leverage to pull herself to her feet. We ran back down the beach toward our siblings, chanting, "We're going to marry you, we're going to bury you!"

Halfway down the beach we dug two shallow grooves like graves, and when the holes were dug my brother Alex lay right down, and Emily ran. Paul chased her and tickled her until she was laughing and crying hard enough to be forced into place.

I scooped the sand onto Emily's stomach very gently and collected seashells to place in a bridal crown around her head.

Alex, lying calmly next to her, said, "Don't worry, Emily, we can always get a divorce." He looked at her, batting his long eyelashes, and smiled.

And then I had an idea.

I looked at Caroline and said, "Now bury us."

Caroline lifted up her arm and pointed to where the waves broke, where the sand was heavy with water.

"There," she said, looking at me, and I knew she'd heard me laugh.

With ten hands we dug two holes, deeper this time and pooling with water. Once we were inside the brothers and sister slapped sand onto our stomachs, heavy dollops of it, cold explosions that turned warm as the sand covered and sucked at us, as the pat, pat, pat of their hands moved over us like muscles. We were being swallowed inside the earth's stomach!

I tried to surrender to its full-body squeeze.

"You're stupid, Caroline," said Paul, kneeling over us and shaking his head.

Then he moved on top of me, bent close, and winked.

And in a second they were gone. Not just Paul, but Emily and even my brother. They left us packed in, the ocean rushing up at our eyes.

At first I decided we were fine. I hated Paul, and decided we were fine. I could wiggle my hips and thought I could slowly work my way out. I knew the story of the people born from the mud of the Nile and I imagined the reverse, a de-evolution—that we might erode and slowly join the ocean, like cocoons the water washed over and hatched into fish. By the time I remembered the horror movie about the adulterous lovers, buried to their necks and left for high tide, Caroline had already started to scream.

Then someone walked up behind us.

Someone with large hairy legs straddled us, towered above us, not as threatening as Zeus, maybe more like the Jolly Green Giant. He took a puff on a cigarette, blew out a thin trail of smoke—the track a jet makes, miles up in the sky.

"What do we have here?" he asked. "What are these specimens washed up by the sea?"

"Dad, dig us out!" Caroline yelled.

"They make strange noises. Gurgle. Gurgle."

He gave us a long puzzled look, exclaimed "Aha!" and dropped to his knees.

It didn't help that Caroline's dad was a scientist.

He worked carefully, dividing the sand along our chests into four even piles, rounding each pile, until we were only heads attached to large floating breasts. He held up several small seashells, rolling them between his fingers, assessing size, and shape, before placing one on each peak.

"Sex correctly identified!" he said, spreading his arms wide as if offering an embrace, but his head was right over mine and I could see a secret pleasure in his smile. I could see it scissoring up through the slit of his lips.

The next day Caroline wouldn't go in the water, nor the day after that. While our brothers and sister went to the beach we spent our time lying on the docks trying to catch crabs with bubblegum attached to the ends of strings. We set the traps by lowering the chewed-up treasure right down to the crabs' doorsteps. When the crabs crawled out and got their claws stuck we reeled them up to the dock, spinning.

"We're probably giving them mini heart attacks," Caroline said. She dropped one into our plastic bucket, made a grimace with her face, and held it over the top of the bucket like a lid.

"Stupid crabs, stupid crabs," she told them. But when one crab's body fell off and we pulled up just a dangling arm she looked disturbed, and scampered down to the rocks to find the rest of it.

"If we hold the body up to the arm it might reconnect," she told me, and I remembered our school nurse, the same nurse who lectured us on the proper uses of maxi pads. She'd once instructed us to save our finger, or any small appendage, in a plastic bag in the event we cut something off. She'd said that the veins and the tissues of the severed parts wouldn't forget each other, they would re-bond, open right back up.

But once Caroline was down on the rocks, she gave up quickly. She climbed back up to the dock, and lay down on her back with her T-shirt strategically bunched. I followed her back up and dumped out the bucketful of crabs, gently, but so she would notice—and let them plop back into the sea. When she didn't respond I put on my roller skates and rode in circles around her so the slats of the dock rumbled under her arms and legs. I performed spins and leaps— I wanted her to be inspired or jealous of how I could be light and powerful, a goddess of the air and rocks and sky. But Caroline had sealed off her energy along her border. Before, her energy had been something I could walk into, feel around me, suck up like a mist. Now it was guarded, and she vibrated it seemed with the effort of just staying separate. Now, she acted like an off-limits sticker, or a pair of fancy jeans. This made me not want to share with her, but to grab what she had like a boy might, to steal it for myself.

I took off my skates and sat down. I put my hand on her stomach and smoothed out her shirt. She pretended I wasn't there so I pretended she was dead and that I was preparing her for a funeral: I brought my fingers up over her face, touched her eyelids and smoothed down her eyebrows. I fanned her hair out around her head, took off my bracelet and set it on her stomach as an offering. I got close and stared down at her; I pressed the tips of my eyelashes into hers. I put my hand on her stomach and made it crawl, slowly, up under her shirt. I thought of measles, chicken pox, red lumps that were contagious. When I touched her nipple it felt like half of a grape, sliding under silk. I said, "See, I'm not afraid of you." I rolled away down the dock and waited to see if she would come back.

Audra

The first time Molly saw her, Audra was throwing herself backward, hooking her knees into the high beam of the jungle gym and flipping. She was upside down, and falling through the air. It was spring in Ohio, the summer heat creeping in. It melted the edges of buildings, turned the ramadas and portables, the large flat cubes of the public school buildings, into shivery holograms. Molly closed and opened her eyes, for the girl wavered as she landed and walked toward her—she could have been the shadow of a bird, or a displaced piece of dream.

Molly chose not to alert her best friend, Cindy Fairchild. Cindy who sat next to her, expertly flipping colored rings from the backs of her hands to the palms.

"My name is Audra," the girl said, stopping five feet away, standing perfectly straight as if held up by strings. She was small and thin and her skin stretched tightly across her face, a little like cooked plastic, Molly thought, as if she'd been stuck in the oven and Shrinky Dinked.

Now Cindy looked up. She wore clip-on hair feathers and they shivered at Audra's presence, expanded like defensive bird wings.

"Stop where you are!" Cindy said. She jumped up and pointed to the border where the cement patio they'd spread their jacks across met the sandbox, the border she and Molly enforced to ward off boys, to protect their best-friendness from other girls. Cindy crossed her arms over her chest, tapped her foot. She gathered herself into making a visible effort at being polite.

"I'm afraid to say that you can't play with us," she said, circling Molly's waist with her arm, including by excluding, in a way that made Molly feel specially chosen, indebted and bound.

Once, on an overnighter, lying on Cindy's plush pink comforter, Cindy told Molly that Molly had a special something—she cocked her head, looked into Molly's eyes, and said, "Hmm, I just don't know what that is yet."

"What does she have to say?" Audra asked, bypassing Cindy and pointing to Molly, who was stuck, thinking about how Audra's blue jeans were rigged up with a nylon belt so they buckled under it and folded into pleats. Audra had a silver embroidered star on her hip pocket, but it had burst open—the threads were the trail the star left behind.

"I talk, she listens. Our teacher Mrs. Clements says that I'm verbal and she's visual, which, contrary to what you might think, doesn't mean she's stupid." As she said this Cindy thrust one hand out and put the other on her hip in a defensive dance move à la the Supremes.

This made Molly feel sleepy. She felt sleepy every time she played with Cindy's jacks—the azure blue hoops, the lovely bright reds, transparent as cherry cough drops. She felt tired about having to keep her own jacks, which were scratched and ugly, hidden in her pocket. She was tired, which was somehow dangerously close to angry, about not being able to wear her chocolate-flavored lip gloss, the one that she spent three months' allowance on. She felt she could not wear this lip gloss because Cindy said it made her lips look like mud.

What she did next felt violent, like a magician pulling a bright red scarf up and out of her throat.

She looked up at Cindy, whose head was backlit by the sun so the blond hairs that escaped her barrettes buzzed in an electric halo. She said, "She can play with us."

With one swift movement, Cindy bent down and made her jacks disappear into her jack sack. She swooped back up, feathers twirling, and left as the bell rang. And when Molly turned to look at Audra whom she had just stood up for, she was gone.

Back in the classroom, at reading time, Cindy chose to partner with Jeani, a new girl whom Molly had seen eyeing Cindy's eraser collection. She'd seen her look at the pink ice-cream cones, the fat rubber hearts, the chocolate bars that actually smelled like chocolate—erasers bought with the money her father the heart surgeon gave her every time he went out of town on important business. Cindy didn't vulgarly flaunt her erasers—instead she kept them lined up along the metal pencil rim inside her desk so everyone could catch glimpses of them when she reached inside to slowly sharpen a pencil.

When class was over, Cindy and Jeani, who was pretty but who Molly was happy to notice had a mole on the tip of her nose the size of a small ant, walked the long linoleum hallway arm in arm.

Out on the playground, the sun was trying to light fire to the grass, great bright patches streaked between the trees, and Audra was running through them, wavering in the humid light, disappearing into shadow. As Molly stepped through the gate in the chain-link fence that surrounded the schoolyard, Audra zoomed past. She stopped five feet in front, turned around, skipped ahead, looked back smiling.

Audra followed Molly home or Molly followed Audra. They took the path through the nicer neighborhood, with the trimmed lawns and hedgerows, where the enchanted air slowed time, suspending white poofs of pollen.

In front of a large pointy house, Audra stopped. "Is that where you live?" She leaned back, looking up, as if at a skyscraper.

When Molly shook her head, Audra shrugged and said, "Too bad."

"Where do you live?" Molly asked, for she secretly hoped Audra lived across the ravine, on the less-nice side of the neighborhood.

"Oh, I travel. I want to become an acrobat," Audra said, and Molly saw Audra in a sequined leotard, spotlit, balancing on a high wire. Even now Audra held out both of her arms, and began to spin. She let go of the rock she held in her hand only when it was impossible to know where it would land. It skimmed past Molly's head like a missile.

"Try it," she said, handing Molly a rock. Molly spun once and threw the rock down the safe path of the sidewalk.

"Cindy thinks you're a chicken," Audra said. She stopped and looked directly into Molly's face, so close that Molly saw she had very small and slightly pointy-looking teeth. She swooped down, picked up another rock, and spun again, and this time Molly spun with her, anticipating all potential points of impact—the sparkly bay window of the big house, the hood of its sleek silver sports car, and suddenly Cindy, on the other side of the street, walking fast and furious—her feathers flying.

Molly saw the rock rise through the air. Inside she called out, "Cindy!" but outside she watched the rock arc and descend with pleasure. It hit the back pocket of the new designer blue jeans, the blue jeans with an embroidered firecracker on one butt cheek. On the other the word "Pow."

Later Molly would discover that these blue jeans had been bought with money Cindy's father gave her mother to take Cindy on long shopping sprees while he was out of town having an affair with his nurse. And later Molly would remember the two images of the firecracker and the "Pow" when her mother told her that Cindy's parents were getting a divorce. Later her mother would whisper this information in her low serious voice, as if it was something she would rather not say but had to. As if it was Molly's duty, especially then, to be a good friend.

Molly's mom was scrubbing the inside of the oven when Molly and Audra walked past the kitchen door. She was waist deep and partially digested. Molly held her finger to her mouth and rushed Audra by, past the bowl of carrot sticks her mom had laid out as unenticing bait.

"Hello?" her mom called out, as Molly softly clicked shut the door of her bedroom. She felt herself tingling, as if she were made of TV, a sassy kid on a sitcom, one of the shows her mother didn't like her to watch.

Molly was excited to show Audra her bedroom in a way she'd never been with Cindy. She showed her the bunk bed and the white shelves that her father built, running around the top of the room. The shelves were lined with stuffed animals, some of whom Molly secretly liked less than others and didn't bring down to the lower bed where she slept. But she could justify this, she thought. The ones she did bring down, Winnie with the missing eye and Fuzzy with the pointed head, were the ugliest, the most forlorn, and as her mother would say, the most in need of her love. Outside of school, in private, Molly tried to be very good.

She climbed up onto her bed, grabbed Fuzzy and Winnie to explain her good-night routine to Audra.

She said, "First I say good night to all of my stuffed animals at once. I say, 'Good night, sweet animals.' Then I say another good night to Fuzzy and Winnie. But I always switch the order so they know I don't think of one of them first, or save the special one for last. That way they know I love them both the same amount but in different ways.

"My mom says she'll always love me but sometimes she doesn't like me very much," she continued. And then Molly told Audra that she always found Fuzzy under the bed, or upside down in a corner, always somehow doing the wrong thing.

"Still," she said, "I don't say good night to him first or last. I say, 'Oh, Fuzzy!' I just feel sorry for him and wonder if he'll ever learn.

"Oh, Audra," she suddenly said, looking at her dirty shoes and worn jeans. Molly reached out to give Audra a hug.

Audra dodged away, walked to the middle of Molly's room, and started to turn in circles. Her tennis shoes had holes in the toes, and looked more dirty against the freshly vacuumed carpet. When she stopped turning she focused on Molly's desk—the wood across the closed top was painted white and buckling a little. It was a desk you opened by pulling on a porcelain knob, a knob with a pink rose encircled by a gold ring. Inside Molly kept her journal of thoughts.

Audra walked toward the rose on the knob and cocked her head as if to see in under its petals. Molly looked too, so closely the petals seem to rustle. The rose was a rose she'd forgotten about—it wasn't the silver star she really wanted. In fact her mother had picked it out; she'd swept down the aisle right past her star, slowed at the rose, and said, "Oh, but this one is so sweet and old-fashioned!"

Audra looked at the knob and squinted her eyes. Molly felt her head grow as big as a bulb, her body shrink to a stem.

Audra wrapped her fingers around it and pulled. Molly wondered if it was because the surface of the desk was painted white that what she kept inside, by contrast, felt dark. As Audra took out the book of thoughts, Molly moved toward her. She clamped her hands onto one end of it, held on but didn't yank it back. Audra ran her hand over the cover like a fortune-teller, hovering over the sparkly stickers, and Molly could feel the thoughts pulsing, rising up. Inside was what she'd written about her brother, and her mother. Audra dropped the book on the floor.

"Eh, probably boring," she said, and walked toward the door. When she opened it, there was Molly's mom. Audra dodged around her and disappeared.

Molly's mom now stood, hands on her hips, taking full advantage of the doorframe. Molly chose not to notice the soot marks on her mother's forehead. She neglected to remember how her mother so eagerly awaited her arrival home that she sometimes appeared to jump out of the clutches of the house and run into the front yard, as if she had been wrestling with it. Instead Molly only saw the you-should-know-what-you-did-wrong-and-I-know-you-know-so-there-is-no-point-in-saying-it look. And although this normally made Molly shrink and stew, today in the humid heat, Molly felt strangely buoyant.

Her mother, regardless of her loneliness, wasn't fair with her rules. She didn't press them on her younger brother whose skateboard ramp collected strange boys, every day. These boys tracked mud into the bathroom, drank from the water glasses and left them broken outside in the dirt. Molly had watched her mother pause, stand and listen to the boys in the alley, through the open kitchen window. She saw the space she gave her brother. She knew that when it was bedtime and after her mother had tucked them in (taking turns with who she said good night to first), her brother would creep out of his room and up onto the couch—pulled by her invisible strings which were so loose that they gathered and pooled under the circle of her reading lamp. Bit by bit he told her about the boys—what he was thinking, his notes on the day.

"Girls," Molly had heard her mother say through the open car window, to Cindy's mom. "They're more difficult."

"Where's Cindy?" her mother now asked.

But Molly had sealed herself off and was reciting the hundreds of rules she was supposed to follow: to not be too smart, for then there wouldn't be enough smartness left over for her brother; to not be an "individual" like the bossy girl in her Brownie troop; to never want to *beat* anyone, for that meant leaving a bruise; to carry her mother around inside of her, packed in tight, like a compass, but to never repeat the things her mother said. She had learned this last rule only a few days ago, when Cindy's mom sat on the couch saying, "Oh, Rachel, all I do is talk about my problems." Molly, who had just entered the room, felt her mother's words leap from her mouth: "That's OK. Some people can't help being self-involved."

"Where's Cindy?" her mother repeated.

Molly shrugged.

"So it's starting," her mother sighed.

"What?" Molly asked.

"The secrets."

And Molly was afraid this was true.

It was only last week that she'd stolen the silverware from the cafeteria. By accident. Molly's mother had given her money for hot lunch, and she was excited to stand in line with Cindy and the kids who carried bills folded into Velcro wallets, kids who didn't have to bring out sandwiches molded into cup shapes around their apples, or bags of oily peanuts. But when lunch was over she didn't know where to put her tray. She tried to set it in a window where a woman was washing dishes, but the woman leaned out and said, "No, no!" and this made her back into an older boy who said, "Watch it!"

Molly slipped her tray onto a folding chair and when she was out on the playground, waiting for Cindy, she realized she still had her spoon and fork in her hand. She whirled around. In front of Cindy she'd already done such stupid things. She'd once laughed so hard she spit Coke all over the white wallpaper with poppies in Cindy's foyer. She sometimes forgot to wear things like socks or underwear, which Cindy had discovered one day when they were changing into bathing suits. And though Cindy often patted her back and said, "Oh, Molly," had even heroically taken the blame for the spit Coke, Molly still felt ashamed.

"You're so weird sometimes," Molly said aloud and startled by her voice, ran to a hidden space at the far edge of the schoolyard and buried the silverware in a thick patch of grass.

The evening of that same day, Molly wanted to tell her mother about the silverware, as her mother bent over to kiss her, and her breath came down into her own. But she hadn't. Instead, she had a nightmare that Jason Monroe, the boy she secretly hated, fell down in the grass and stood up with the fork wedged into his forehead.

The day after Audra's visit and Molly's standoff with her mom, Molly stood in the hot-lunch line. Again. At breakfast neither she nor her mother had apologized, but her mother had pressed a dollar bill into her hand, a gift to show that her mom was the good one, willing to make concessions.

At lunch, Cindy was sitting with Jeani, and Molly took the only space available, at a table of older boys and Jason Monroe.

"Looks like Cindy has a new best friend," Jason said. Jason Monroe had called her slow, and fatface. He'd told her that her father, who coached their soccer team, was a loser because he gave everyone a chance to play every position. Molly smiled at Jason Monroe. Her mother had told her to kill her enemies with kindness and in fact Jason Monroe would die in high school, along with two other boys, their car flipping four times before skidding off a highway and into a ravine.

After lunch, the stack of plastic lunch trays was back in its regular place. Molly returned her tray and walked along the rows of lunch tables. Here, clusters of friends formed in packs, and Cindy slipped her arm slowly around Jeani's shoulder. Molly kept walking, out through the glass doors leading to the playground, out and over the basketball courts, across the soccer field, until she was nearly at the edge of the playground and saw movement, a figure behind the well of trees. She rushed forward, wanting to surprise Audra, but as her pace quickened her grip tightened around something smooth and cool, her thumb pressed in, and her finger curled up over tines. And then there was Audra at the base of a tree, smiling and holding up last week's fork and spoon.

After that, Audra appeared only two more times that Molly could remember.

Once, after school, Molly passed through the sandbox and saw Audra walking across the top bars of the jungle gym, up against the blue sky as if she were walking along a train track with widely spaced rungs, extended across a bridge, over water. Boys had gathered below her and they held their breath, or some, like Jason Monroe, jeered at her, waited for her to fall. But Audra walked fast and smooth. The wind came up under her hair and raised it all in one piece like a tilting metal bell. Thin transparent strings were holding her up. She didn't need to concentrate. When she reached the last rung, she stepped gingerly into the air, but leaned back so her calves, butt, back, and head hit the last rung, boom, boom, boom, all the way down. Her feet took forever to reach the sand, and she landed in a crouching position, her hair flipped over her face.

Molly ran up and placed a hand on her shoulder. She thought of the horror movie she'd seen at Cindy's house—of the girl whose face ballooned on her head and spun on its axis. But when Audra raised her head her face was miraculously clear, her eyes a hard bright blue. She smiled at Molly and her cheeks were almost rosy.

Later that week, Molly searched for Cindy after school. Their mothers, unaware of the girls' secrets, had arranged a play date. Molly found Cindy leaning against the cement play tunnel fully armored, and with sidekick Jeani. Cindy wore her jeans with the swan on the small pocket; her lips were slick with watermelon lip gloss, and the beautiful barrette woven with lavender ribbons floated against her hair.

"You're supposed to come home with me," Molly said.

"My mom and dad are getting a divorce."

"Oh," Molly said.

Cindy leaned in toward Molly and for a second, Molly felt her fear, and knew the sun was melting and making things unrecognizable. She understood her armor, how the feathery hair gear lifted her up above the school buildings and neighborhoods, up above her parents, although not high enough. She knew how outfits held her together though not forever and entirely. Cindy was slipping from between her seams.

Molly held out her hand but Cindy stepped back.

"I won't come if she comes," she said, pointing to Audra, who had appeared, soundlessly, at Molly's side.

"It's because I'm a freak," Audra said, whispering in Molly's ear. Turning to Cindy she said, "But then again, only bad girls have parents who get divorced."

Audra skipped in front of Molly all the way home.

This time, when they arrived, Molly's mother had set a nice trap.

"Come in," she said. "Don't you girls want to make some cookies?" She gripped and raised a bag of chocolate chips in her hand and held it up, smiling.

"No," Audra said, "I want to play with her things."

Molly avoided looking at her mother, for whom this was a "gotcha" moment. She knew it wasn't polite to say "no" to an adult, and that it was worse to say "her," as if it didn't really matter who Molly was, as if she could have been any girl, as long as she had "things."

"Where do your parents live, Audra?"

"No one cares that I'm here," Audra said.

"But that's not what I asked," said Molly's mother.

Audra shrugged. She pulled Molly's hand and skipped down the hall. She whispered, "Adults ask me about my parents, but they don't really care because I'm not that cute." Audra turned her head toward Molly's mother and batted her eyes—but like a malfunctioning doll's, one of her eyes stuck open and the other batted too fast.

In the bedroom they climbed to the top bunk and Audra resumed her assessment of Molly's possessions. She ran her fingers across Molly's animals, and made her way to her only doll: plump, pinafored Alice in Wonderland. She unsnapped the button at the back of her dress. She took the clothes off slowly and asked, "Is there anything inside?"

She popped off a leg and shook Alice. Then Audra moved both hands over her, took her hair in her fist, gently popped off her arms, her legs, her head, as if she were only folding her up and she would spring back to life, renewed and different and more alive.

"You never know a person until you look inside," she said in a voice like Molly's mom's.

She turned to Fuzzy next, upside-down-in-the-corner Fuzzy, the one who would never learn. She wiggled her finger inside the small patch on his head where the webbing was revealed, the fur worn away.

Molly grabbed hold of Fuzzy's legs and yanked. When Fuzzy broke free she heard a pop. Audra's right eye started blinking fast again. Audra held up her hand and said, "Wait, I'll be nice."

But Molly was backing down the stairs of her bunk.

She was out in the hallway, and then moving through the kitchen. She walked to the backyard, through abandoned garden projects and around through the alley to the front yard, where her mom had been painting a bench. She went back through the house, picking up her pace, and into her parents' bedroom. She yelled into the bathroom, flipped back the shower curtain. She circled the house one more time but her mother, who was always everywhere and on top of her, was gone.

Back in the hallway, Molly closed her eyes. She whispered, "I'm sorry for the secrets," and then her mother reappeared, standing at the other end.

She cried, "No!" and launched forward into Molly's bedroom.

Inside Molly's bedroom, Cindy and Jeani had also appeared. Along with her mother they stood staring, open mouthed, at the bunk bed. Audra stood on the top bunk. Her back to them, the dirty heels of her tennis shoes dipped over the edge of the mattress. Then she was falling—her body perfectly straight, as if she were playing "light as a feather, stiff as a board," the game of slumber parties, in which a girl lies down in the dark, squeezes her muscles tightly, and trusts her friends' fingers to lift and hold her. And at first Audra seemed held. She descended in slow motion, a combination of falling and floating, until she landed, boom, in the circle of their feet.

And then Molly rejoined her mother, and rejoined Cindy. She even joined Jeani who was just Molly's height, and who Molly was beginning to notice had an interesting sense of style. Together it was none of them bending down to touch Audra. It was none of them telling her to stay still in case there were broken bones. It was none of them stopping her when she sat up, eyes wide open, and said matter-of-factly, "I'm leaving now."

It was all of them watching as Audra turned to Molly in passing and said, "You're not such a good girl, you know."

And then she was almost gone.

Molly thought of Audra every time her mother brought up Cindy. For a while this happened about twice a week. Cindy and her mom had moved from their house to an apartment, Cindy had switched schools, yet Molly's and Cindy's moms' friendship had grown stronger. There were long conversations on the telephone in which her mom would say, "Oh, that sounds terrible, a nightmare! I'm so sorry for you, Helen, it's just so unfair." And after each call Molly's mom would look strangely satisfied, and Molly knew she could expect an argument.

"I'd like you to call Cindy," her mother would say. And Molly, who was deep in a new friendship with Jeani, always said no.

"You have something to learn about friendship," her mother said one day, after a fresh refusal. And Molly said, "Your only friends are people you can take pity on," the words hot, bright, and only half hers. They were also Audra's, who had remained partially inside of her and was spinning, a blur of arms and legs, a tiny tornado, rising up out of her stomach and making Molly dizzy, as if she herself were spinning, being lifted and carried, she didn't know where.

Details

We're driving up the side of his mountain in his red BMW. He's wearing flip-flops and I'm not sure they're right for the occasion. He's supposed to seduce me, and I'm supposed to be seducible, but it's a plan I don't like to admit, and it's less important than the feeling of the tropical drink, and rising up through hills away from Los Angeles. I'm rising, to look through the window he has for a wall, to sit inside a house with low-lit lamps, guitar music, and magazines he's told me are smart.

He pours us wine from a box.

"I've been wanting to do this for a long time," he says.

"Oh, right, this," I say, pretending I know.

He moves onto the couch, beckons me over, and switches to a jungle-cat way of moving I guess he picked up in the acting classes he's told me about.

"You make me shy," he says, and I say, "I'm shy too," although I don't think he needs it. He crouches toward me with his wide shoulders, and I think, stop, but instead point to a framed print of a girl by a well with a cracked pitcher and a halo of mussed-up hair. She looks younger than me, and I don't like her here, in this space where I'm trying to be my full twenty-three years, a smart young woman, if not yet an intellectual equal.

But he kisses me and I forget.

I also forget to be happy that he's kissing me.

I forget that I've actually made it, because the kiss feels weird, and I wonder if it's because I'm not paying attention. I try to feel the drink feeling, the rising, the way he put his hand on my back in the blue glow of the restaurant. Instead, I think that size is at least important when it comes to tongues, because his is large and fills my mouth and I think, if I just had a little pocket of air, some room for atmosphere.

But it's hard to say this to your professor. Especially when you're about to graduate with a liberal arts degree, don't know what you're doing next, except that you'd like to do what he does, though with less bitterness. It's hard when you're good at living inside your internal world, and when for the last three months most of that world has been wondering, gathering hints, and inventing around the possibility of him. Now, you have to match your internal idea of him to the suddenness of the external, such things as the jungle cat, smell of alcohol, and tongue. And there is a gap, a wide gap, that must be filled with images of lingering in this beautiful house and spotting the peacocks that sit in the trees.

He's told you about the peacocks in conference. How they make strange sounds late at night, and last night he called at twelve o'clock, just to give some feedback on a story, and his voice sounded thick and lonely and you didn't really know why, but you could imagine.

He stops and everything gets quiet. He tilts his head and says, "Listen, do you hear the peacocks?"

It's a small gargling sound, like someone drowning on purpose. He bounces off the couch, stands with his feet apart, tilts his head back, and imitates the call. I remember how he told me that all great writers are addicts, how he hints about his "brain pills," does five Diet Pepsis a day, coffee, but not mixed with sugar. I don't know if this means he's a true writer or vulnerable to peer pressure. And when he swoops me up in both of his arms, like a baby? or a bride?, I think, OK, let's just go with it. I think it's part of getting to love.

He carries me into the bathroom and lets me use his toothbrush. I add it to the list of things we've shared. A list of things that so far have allowed us to be both connected and separate. A ballpoint pen, opinions on movies, two straws in the same large drink. I start to feel brave from the accumulation and say, "I've never had sex."

He moves out from behind me and takes his hand off my shoulder. "Well, that's"—he pauses—"something." I feel the momentum of my list thud. He slaps one hand down on the counter and looks at me flat, without the jungle-cat gaze, and says he's surprised. He walks around the room more stiffly now, and moves his arms so it looks like he's trying to shake his muscles out. He says, "I'm proud of you," and I say, "I'm not." Then he goes into a private place I haven't seen before, lifts up and whispers, "So that's why."

"Why what?"

"That's why you came up here."

I would like to add, "And you invited me," but he's coming toward me again, faster and more romantic. He lifts my hand and kisses one of my fingers, and I think this is the way he talks about stories, that once he's discovered the conflict, the resolution should be inevitable. He leads me toward his big window, and looks out. His eyes seem to focus on one tiny light in the LA skyline. When I look there are too many to focus only on one—all shaking and shimmering like a disco runway, or disembodied evening dresses. I wonder if he's been trying to piece me together by noting my bulky denim jacket, my soft short dress, tiny earrings, but red. He must know I'm dressed in contradictions not because I'm sophisticated or playing games, but because I'm unsure. He thinks that he can be my resolution.

He bounds over the bed and pushes a button on his answering machine, he puts on a deep whispery voice, comes and slides his hands from my shoulders to my hips, squats, touches the backs of my knees, then my ankles so he's got the breadth of me, pops back up, lifts me, puts me into bed with my dress still on, lies on top of me and says, "We'll go slow."

I can go slow without him.

I try to think about my dress and how in the restaurant it felt tight against my ribs and opened at the bottom, how I felt excited in front of the aquariums, like I was in an unknown element, wasn't sure where I was swimming, but could see enough details—the plastic pineapple lights, the blue and yellow flanks of fish, and now, wait, his leopard-print underwear? I think about how my friends would relish this detail and I start to feel the first piece of a story. I wonder how it might build and fill and change in everyone's ears. I wonder what my friend Alice will hear, who looked at me straight and said, "Don't do it, Melissa."

He has all his clothes off.

I ask, "What about my dress?"

"Leave it on."

"Why?"

"It will protect you from me."

But I don't need to be protected, I think. I've been accumulating—adding details. Growing means opening and I've been opening to him and having to incorporate new information into my original idea of him, and I would like to see this experience as an incorporable piece. I say, "I want to feel close to you." But he isn't listening. He's bending my knees.

He says, "I like a little obstacle."

And he pushes in and his head has dropped off to the side and I feel stupid just lying there, so I try to join by adding observations. "This sort of feels like riding a horse," I say, and he says, "Yes." I say, "I feel like one of those things that quarterbacks run into," and he says, "Yessss," and he's going fast and he's heavy and his eyes are closed and I see that's so he doesn't have to look at me. I ask, "Could we take a break?" and my voice sounds funny, like a chipped-off part of it, and it hurts, but he said it might hurt. Right after he pushed in.

I try to be a sport. I remember the time my dad said I was a wimp because I wouldn't let him pull my tooth out. I try to think of it like getting a loose tooth pulled. I'll buck up; I have to learn sometime. But then I remember that I didn't let my dad pull my tooth. I walked around for weeks with it dangling, and when it finally fell out I tied a ribbon around it and kept it in my jewelry box. I feel myself concentrating like that tooth is in my stomach.

I say it louder. "I want to stop."

He stops, gets up from the bed, and walks into the other room. I wonder what he's doing. I hear him peeing. I hear him running water. He comes back and I'm lying on my stomach and he lies on top of me and says, "I know you wanted to stop, but sometimes little boys . . ." He pushes inside again and I'm back down in the mattress. I try to think that it's better face down—it eliminates any question of my performance. But mostly I don't think, I hold on to the pillow and listen. I try to keep my head up because it's hard to breathe.

In the morning he looks embarrassed. He brings me dried figs and cheese arranged in a circle on a china plate. He wants to sit on the patio so we can look down on his landlord's trees. I pick up a fig and examine it.

"Why don't you eat?" he asks. I'm thinking that it looks like a part of the male anatomy. He has half a fig in his mouth and he chews it very slowly. He watches me watching him and smiles.

He's careful with me, now that he's reached closure. Now I'm something left over, a different person, probably a little dangerous. I'm like one of those strange out-of-the-blue images that are initially so exciting but must be eliminated when they begin to take on lives of their own. Or maybe kept on file. I wonder how many other girls he keeps on file. I push my chair out and walk to his room to get my things and to search for one last detail. There's his already-made bed, with the covers smoothed over. There are six red flashes on his answering machine that weren't there last night.

We walk down a zigzagging path through the gardens. In one of the trees I think I see a flash of blue feathers, but it's the underside of leaves in the wind. The trees are full and shimmering, and the leaves are big enough to wipe across a face. I walk ahead of him, decide I want one. I go down, and I'm about to pass in front of a window when he yells, "Stop," and I stop the way he didn't, the way he tells me to stop my stories, to go back, revise, to never get out of control. He runs down, saying, "I'll get it." When he comes back up he's smiling. "Professor Pater lives there." He knocks me in the arm with his elbow and covers his mouth as if to conceal an "oops."

The ride down the hill is too slow. He takes his time, leaning with the curves, whistling through his teeth at his movement. I fix on my token, my leaf with the turquoise-blue back, and let myself float into the realm of possibility. I imagine that the car has stopped, that he's already kissed me and touched my hand conspiratorially, and that I'll have stashed in my bag details for later use.

I imagine how I'll step out at the pet store, where we started with me pretending to stare into the aquarium of goldfish while he moved in behind. No, this time I'll start without him. I'll walk out of the pet store, past the coffee shop, and bakery. I'll stop in front of the bungalow with the plastic pink flamingo, the unexotic, out-of-context, brilliant pink flamingo with the tiny wise eye. Forget the peacocks. I'll start there.

When Maggie
Thinks of Matt

When Maggie thinks of Matt she thinks of an Edward Weston photograph of a large plaster mug in the middle of a desert with the word coffee painted onto it as an enticement. She thinks of misplaced, mismatched old things, such as the mildewed movie house just up the street from her apartment in the neighborhood she didn't know was dangerous, and of the movie star he said she could be. She thinks of the building facades in downtown Syracuse, gray and leaking soot, of the inside of the old opera house, opulent with decay. She thinks about his bad teeth and tiny handwriting—squared and old-fashioned like the keys on a typewriter. The woman with a baby on the porch next door, who looks at her so she can't look back. She thinks of what she can't remember—of petticoats, green silk undergarments, hospital sheets, carved mermaids shedding their scales, and overripe fruit. She thinks of her privileged longing for experience.

It's strange to her that she used to touch him. It makes her shiver to remember. Even then it made her buzz with a mixture of excitement and revolt. Yet it was she who called him up, because he was smart—really smart, she thought, and forty-five years old. She said, "Come over for dinner," and he arrived with a bottle of wine and a smile that set all his wrinkles into high relief, made his face crack open with pleasure, made him look terrible, the way she looked as a small girl, smiling so hard her lips climbed up over her teeth so only her gums showed. She remembers thinking, oh no, he's like me, and, this will never work.

She remembers trying not to look at him during dinner. She'd forgotten his skin was crepe, his face not strong boned, and that his eyes were dull, with a brown ironlike spot, similar to the surface of an old toy where the white lacquer had been rubbed away. But he kept looking at her and catching her looks, crinkling up his face and smiling. His energy was so strong, she thinks, a little like a wound trying to heal; a desperate sucking, as if she were air and light. How could she resist being pulled into all that intensity?

Still, it's embarrassing to recall herself as the person who was flattered by his way of looking—the winks she mistook for wisdom but now understands as a simple recognition of her loneliness, and a romantic ploy. He had a way of looking that said, "We're both sad souls alone in the universe"—which is exactly what she would have wanted him to see—her sadness that came in and out, that she thinks of now as a quirky gene, but once entertained as deep, once wanted someone to unearth, in order to show everyone how she might be a Sylvia Plath, or a young Virginia Woolf, under the youthful pleasure of her looks.

But that was ten years ago.

Last week an old friend told her that somewhere in that space, Matthew had been driving, he'd slipped off an icy road and died.

So she remembers carefully, her boldness with him that first night, how she took him up to the attic because it was dusty and full of antiques and forbidden by her landlord, which made it more erotic than the candy-colored couch under the windowsill covered with bright glass bottles, where he would surely look too old and decayed. The attic contained the full-length mirror she'd once stripped in front of, which held her body in a flattering light, made her small breasts look bigger, her boy-frame yellow, buttery, and full.

Climbing the attic stairs, she remembers becoming aware that having a man behind her could be sexy. She'd seen it in a movie, the slightly affected pivot of the hips, the surprise of being taken from behind.

And as she climbed his wrinkledness vanished. He became a dark shadow, taller, until, in the attic, his shadow dropped. The attic was brighter than she'd remembered, lit up with fluorescent light. And he hesitated, turned stiff and self-protective.

And this is where she fills in what she wants him to have been thinking.

He might have been thinking that he was twenty years older, had two children, and liked to dress in women's clothing for erotic pleasure. He might have been thinking about how this would be used as evidence against him by his ex-wife in an upcoming custody case. He was probably thinking that he loved his children, but had spent thirty years of his life keeping secrets and cultivating self-destructive behavior, and now that he was out in the open, falling apart, here was this girl-woman, bright—like Mary Tyler Moore, the can-do type, like all the girl-women he fell for and wanted to be. And this is when, she thinks, that laugh of deep pleasure and sadness bubbled up, as if he were saying, "Ah, I am finally at my most tragic."

And if it weren't for his pause and the mystery of this laugh, she might not have put her hand on his chest and leaned into his jacket, into all his layers like dusty bird feathers, or old books at the Salvation Army. If he hadn't hesitated and she hadn't leaned in, she wouldn't have taken on the form of a prepubescent girl from one of those books, with a large candy-apple face, and he might not have decided he would be romantic, different from the boys with the instant erections, like his son, those uncontrollable lightning-bolt erections that he wasn't sure he could have anymore anyway. That were never the register of love. And yes, he would love her. He was the type to fall for faces, to keep his mind away from the responsibilities he didn't plan on having, and the mistakes, oh, the big mistakes of his life. Yes, he'd show her something different. This girl with the changeable face, the seriousness and lightness, this constant shifting, like light on glass. He'd show her gentleness from a man; at least, that would be his intention.

So he said, "Can I kiss you?"

And she remembers that she didn't like the taste of his lips, his tongue felt too thin, and his breath had the bitterness of a bad diet. It might have ended there. If she hadn't caught sight of their figures in the full-length mirror, hadn't seen the way his arm rested on her back, and the glow of her own skin, then the way his long coat enfolded her. The way he flipped his collar up like a vampire, or a detective—half comfort, half danger.

When he caught her watching he turned her toward the mirror and said, "Look," with sudden delight, talking to her as if she were his daughter, whom he saw only on holidays. He said, already with misplaced pride of ownership, "Don't you look just like a picture."

*   *   *

When Maggie thinks of Matthew she remembers driving through narrow streets, through sleet that shrouded the car so they could barely see out, and how the whole world was plastic upholstery, cigarette smoke, and melancholy pop like her own, but two decades older, so crackly and more romantic with feedback. She remembers how the smoke in the car was the only thing that made stepping out into the sleet refreshing, and how hard she'd worked to not be disappointed that Syracuse was actually pretty far from that other city in New York.

She tried to compensate by exploring the insides of the old buildings like the opera house. The bank buildings from when the city was bustling and rich. She walked downtown, lifting her face to look at the grimaces of the gargoyles on the Catholic church. And now she'd tired of the effort and Matt was happy to drive her to strip malls instead. He had no artistic qualms about drinking coffee in brightly lit chain bookstores—even if these were stores that would never sell the kind of books he wanted to write.

But they were not lovers—they just pretended to be. This was because, after only one date, Matt, realizing the full tragedy of his situation (breakup of a marriage, potential loss of a daughter, and full responsibility for a teenage son) could not help but read his poem, announcing to the world (that was really their small circle of acquaintances) that he used to borrow his sister's skirts, and that his son had just come upon his secret—a box of mail-ordered women's clothing, lipsticks, and perfumes.

And although the poem was a hit with their peers, she was suspicious of the way he'd thrust a copy into her hand before the reading so she wouldn't be "shocked" but could decide then and there if she ever wanted to see him again. She couldn't help but find this crisis of their "love" presumptuous, and the catharsis of the reading itself a little self-indulgent. But despite her suspicion, and even though he publicly grabbed her arm after the reading, she liked it a little because some of the others—the ex–sex worker, the transgendered woman—suddenly looked at her with more respect. She liked it a little because the whole situation *was* so dramatic and unlike anything she thought she would experience.

And she was lonely. She had acquaintances. But some of them let her know in subtle ways that she was too young, too midwestern, to be very interesting. In defense she'd tried wearing 1950s librarian glasses and combat boots to show she could at least be complicated. For Halloween she dressed to show she understood that beauty could be a trap. She was Marilyn Monroe with a pill stuck to her face and worse-than-usual bedhead. Or she plastered her hair to her head with a whole container of gel and was a drowned Natalie Wood.

But then she had to wonder who she really was, now that she was invoking alienation. And her enactments of female victimhood were making her feel a little spooked, more fearful than usual of walking home through her neighborhood at night.

She'd begun to look twice at shadows, to fumble her keys in locks, and to frequently feel that someone was following her. She hoped it was real, and that it was just Matthew. Matt knew her routine. He watched her enough to pass her a napkin at a party if she needed one, or to wink at her from across the room when she didn't know who to talk to. Maybe, to take the edge off, she'd confront the seduction. She'd be a brave girl—she'd turn around and look him in the rusty eye.

So she made a sort of compromise. She made a list of things they could do together and places they could go, and at these places they could talk about her screenplays, movies, or music, and she could grill him about his past life, his ex-wife, son and daughter, but he couldn't ask her about *her* past life. He had to make guesses about her based on her behavior alone.

As for places, they could go to the bakery bused by the mentally disabled and the bar on Queen Street he'd shown her, but only after 11:00 PM, and preferably on a rainy night because then it was like being inside a jeweled chamber, tucked into the first floor of a massive old building that had once been a grand hotel. Now the bar was the only part of the structure that felt alive; it was the overworked heart of the dying city, and here she was writing her film noir screenplay, for when she walked into the bar's heat she felt the cold, and Death more acutely, pressing in on all sides, up against the deep red booths and windows that wrapped around, so they could look out to the street and see the neon beer signs light up the puddles—red, green, and blue.

They had conversations that went something like this. He'd say, "What do you think makes a good pop song?" and she'd say, "Mystery, having enough open space in the lyrics so anybody can fill in their life." And if she'd said that, he would probably have said, "I'm not good at open space. It makes me shake." And she would say, "I know, you won't leave me alone, you like things claustrophobic," and he would say, "You are smart, aren't you?"—eyes twinkling, slipping into seductive, because he knows she'll say, "You mean you thought I was stupid," after which he will laugh, "Ha," in that staccato way, finger on a typewriter key, because he likes to set her off, and then say something like, "You should have been around for punk," or "You should have seen this or that."

And she will think he's patronizing, she'll think it's a double standard that older men can fall for younger women but not vice versa, and she will not want to change the subject from her smartness, but she'll be curious about how she could be punk. He'll tilt his head back, smoking now, satisfied to have her attention—he'll be lost in interior monologue, like a slowly chugging engine.

She'll have read more of his poetry by then, his words like little pieces of metal, like braces, or outmoded machine parts. Sometimes like charms. She'll be getting impatient for him to say something insightful, to look deep, to figure her out. And then he'll say, "You could have been punk because you'd look good in tight pants."

And she will think this goes too far.

She'll think she has liked him not for his body. In fact, she has liked him despite it. She tells him, "Don't say that," because his body frightens her. She doesn't really trust his so-called desire because he likes her for who he says she's like—Mary Tyler Moore or a neurotic Doris Day. And sometimes she thinks it's a vampire desire—she thinks he wants to steal her body and put it on. But he changes the subject because a song by the Byrds, or, no, the Turtles, is on the jukebox and they're drinking and their moods are always quick to change.

He says, "No, I take it back. You're a jangle-pop kind of girl." And she says, "What's that?" always with a tone of suspicion when she doesn't know something. He says, "California pop, sunshine, but with a melancholy underneath like Mama Cass. Dream a little dream, that aching thing, you know, like Marian the Librarian, ah man, singing to the stars." And her breath catches in her throat because she knows that song—"Goodnight, my someone, goodnight, my love." He says, "The sadder but wiser girl for me," smiling like crazy because he's on a roll. And suddenly she asks, "What do you think it takes to fall in love?" She's worried that this hasn't happened to her yet. He looks and sees she wants to answer, and leans back to listen. She says, "I don't think it's possible. I think we always put ourselves onto the other person, our own idea of them. We smother them with ourselves before we can get to know them." He says, "Man, you're tough," which she likes. Then he shifts in his seat, his arms stretch out along the vinyl booth, a cigarette makes his hand graceful. He says, "Love is looking carefully enough at someone to see what they want you to see." And she thinks, oh yes, and he's got her there, again.

But he was not so smooth and confident all the time. He called her three or four times a day to say that if they couldn't truly be together he would stop calling. He called her to say he couldn't be with someone who didn't know herself—who was so confused—then he called her back and apologized. He'd explain how his shrink said she'd probably given him something, or he wouldn't have wasted his time. He said his shrink didn't think he was as self-destructive as he liked to think he was, and now, in order to prove this to himself, he was ready to let her go, so "Goodbye," he said, and she'd wait on the line and he would wait, and then partly to tease him, and partly because she was jealous of how often he talked about his shrink, she might have said something like, "OK, and I'm sure this is easier now that you're in love with your shrink too." And at this, he would have either laughed and agreed, or, if drinking, become angry and yelled. One night he did yell. In public—reaching across the table full of people and pulling her up by her arm. Then she knew it was over, for a few days, a week, maybe it was a month, or, anyway, until she got hit by the car.

According to Matthew there was a reason she got hit. She was "clogged," he said, not letting her real emotions to the surface. The accident was a warning, a sign from the universe to let go and accept herself for who she was at the moment—i.e., in love with him.

No, she said.

She granted him that it was cloudy that day rather than clear, that she often felt floaty and unreal and it was true that she'd recently taken to driving through icy streets listening to her sad pop music, bittersweet harmonies, in order to feel she was going someplace and to get herself to cry. But it was also true that the accident happened after she'd finally faced up to all her unpaid parking tickets. In fact, it happened as she was walking out of the DMV. The sky had opened up—the last thing she remembered was a burst of starlings, dividing, cutting open the clear blue sky.

No, she told him later. It was random. The hit was no gentle nudge or warning from the universe—it was too close of a call. In a world with a master plan she wouldn't have almost died at a down time, she would have had a proper ending.

"You're a dark girl, darker than me," he said, which flattered her artistic sensibilities even though she wasn't sure it was true.

She thought of death and decay too often, having been carefully raised on ways to avoid it—on *drink your milk, look both ways, brush and floss your teeth*. She was pretty sure this only made her neurotic in a typical way. Of course, she also thought of death at all the happiest moments of her life because at those moments she wasn't scared of it. She could face it. Things had worked out, wound up, had found a well-deserved ending, and at those moments perhaps death was preferable to moving on; because a happy ending meant there would have to be another beginning, another exhausting struggle and search for closure.

And she doesn't, even now, remember the accident. She remembers waking up in the hospital to a nurse who rolled her eyes when she asked what had happened, and later discovering she'd already asked, several times, each time forgetting the answer. She remembers looking at her face in the bathroom mirror and discovering that no one had wiped off the blood, thinking she should be disturbed but noting how it made her appear eerily glamorous, and wondering if the experience would give her more edge. She remembers feeling strangely uninhibited, wanting to have sex with the CAT scan technician who called her "sweetie." She remembers the tepid feeling of the sheets against her skin, as if they were partially alive after having been soaked and washed through multiple cycles of sweat, shit, blood, and amniotic fluid, and wondering if now she could really be an artist, if in coming close to death she'd crossed a barrier. Might all the ideas, words, and images be held inside those trembling sheets?

But the next day a doctor told her she'd be fine. She'd have a bruised face, achiness all over, a blank space of one-half of a day—the actual accident, her near-death experience, was gone.

And now here was Matt, rumpled from sleeping in the waiting room, high on his imagined rescue and gazing into her face, which was swollen enough to give him the satisfaction of feeling what she thought might be real pity and fear.

She said, "Please, don't think you're in love with me because I'm wounded."

But he stayed anyway, and perhaps in punishment for her meanness, his prophecy that something underlying, deep, and structural was wrong with her seemed to come true.

She remembers her fear of coming home from the hospital and being poisoned both by mold from the leaky ceiling and by peeling lead paint. She remembers remembering her childhood allergy to dust (for she didn't own a vacuum) and wondering if the allergy had turned to asthma, or valley fever because she couldn't breathe right, had to think about getting the inhale in proper proportion to the exhale. Had to think about this all the time. She remembers her fear of falling down stairs, and the fuzzy jacket that no matter where it was laid kept turning into a large black bear. She remembers seeing a silhouette of Nosferatu with his pointy ears and evil talons outside her shower door, her suddenly terrifying neighborhood where one murder had occurred, and the children who wouldn't get out of the way of her car, who sensed her fear, walked slowly and looked at her through the windshield.

And was she able to write her screenplays right here at the edge like a Sylvia Plath, an Anne Sexton, or Matt's favorite, Robert Lowell?

The answer to that was no.

What it really came down to was that she needed a companion. She needed someone to stay the night with her but to sleep on the couch. Matt would do it. Matt would take his shoes off and sleep in his clothes. He'd tuck his bag in an out-of-the-way place and fold his jacket over it. In the morning he'd be up and the blankets would be folded. She'd be happy to see him and they'd drive to the bakery bused by the mentally disabled, who wouldn't look at them strangely, as if to ask, "What is this young girl doing with this man who is clearly falling apart?" And they would talk about music and movies.

Their conversations would go something like this:

He would tell her that she should finish her degree and move someplace new. Really, she was full of spunk. She needed a change of place and so did he. He could meet her in Colorado or San Francisco, his dream city. She would remind him that he was trying to gain custody of his daughter from his crazy ex-wife, whose craziness she was beginning to doubt. He would smile and say, "Oh, I forgot about that." Would say, "You know I have a big heart for my children," to reassure her. He would wink and say, "See, my fantasy girl, see what you do to me."

And she would be kind, she'd say, "I can play along."

She gave him a Björk cassette. He gave her Laurie Anderson.

And then the snow had melted and the daylilies were startling, lining the roads as surely as miniature palm trees. It was summer and he was her best friend.

So the idea crept into her head, because of these things, and because she was sitting in the right pose, in the windowsill of her empty bedroom as he walked by the door. He was helping her pack to move out, was carrying an armful of clothing and had his trench coat on, had that element of detective/vampire with the collar turned up— half comfort, half danger.

She watched him carry her things, saw how careful he was, and his gesture, when the green silk slip fell out of his hand, his quick bend to pick it up, and to cover it—its green like a papaya, like mermaid skin, like the painted scales on the mermaids in the old movie house. When he set his hand on top of it she called his name and he looked up, embarrassed, and saw her sitting in that position, legs open like a boy's, elbow on knee. She knew he saw her as smart and sexy, a round-faced girl with a bra strap showing—a clever Sandra Dee. She knew he paid attention to what she wanted him to see.

And she was already hot from the sunlit space in the window. He said, "Look at you, you look just like a picture."

And she remembers weighing how much she wanted to be touched against not wanting to touch back; although, as she started to peel off his layers like book pages, like dusty bird feathers, she got carried away with the momentum, perhaps carried away with her own bravery. As she peeled, his forty-five years dropped, and he was a child to her, so delicate and white, like parchment paper, like a ghost, like a hospital sheet.

She remembers:

She covers them both in blankets and holds him. She guides his hands over her belly and breasts because she's impatient, wants him to have an erection, and doesn't think he'll get one: he's too cold, and his heart is beating too fast. She works his hands over her body, with her own movement, as if she's the one who has slipped inside of him and he's strangely, after all his huffing and monologuing, her puppet.

When she's done she doesn't ask him what he wants. She won't let him put the green silk slip on his own body. She never did broach the subject of his desires.

When she thinks of Matthew she thinks of her journey west, of being only twenty-five and wanting to be a cowgirl, riding glamorous and in slow motion on a moving neon sign. She thinks of red lipstick, the tubes he secretly mail-ordered, how he once asked to watch her put it on, and how she told him no, but that maybe in the future he could get his own vagina. She thinks of black and white. Of curvy ice-covered streets cutting through snow, of all the times her car skidded and slipped and barely missed parked cars, of his own steady driving, of how she admired his pace. She thinks of every kind of disaster—of objects piercing the thinnest of substances, penetrating gauze and silk—of losing and regaining her boundaries. She thinks of his five-page single-spaced and typed letters, in which he said beautiful things, mean things, got carried away in his coffee-and-smoke-induced passion, envisioned her any way he wanted because she wasn't there to respond. She knows that sleeping with him was selfish. She wishes she could tell him that she believes he did love her. She wishes she could tell him that she had loved him too.

*   *   *

When she thinks of Matthew she hopes his accident had good timing. She imagines he was looking at a hawk flying off along the side of the road, feeling romantic and connected to nature. She imagines that the sky was blue and he was "unclogged," that his car was warm, and that a pair of his daughter's mittens from her last visit sat on the dashboard. She imagines he was thinking in his bright metallic words, writing, his mind clicking away like typewriter keys. She imagines he was listening to a good song with a deep bruised voice, and the sudden high rising of jangling guitars.

Jill, or The Big Little Lady

The little lady inched open the door of her pickup truck using both of her Barbie-sized feet, and in a grinding effort of lower body strength flung the door wide. She jumped to the curb, barely cleared the gutter, and landed next to a hazy rain puddle—ringed with rainbows of gasoline, studded with sticky blue and pink islands of gum.

A man standing at the curb smoking dropped his cigarette. He was smitten at the sight of the small figure flying through the air. The lady watched the cigarette fall toward her, a burning timber, imagining how it might ignite the gasoline-infused puddle and burst it into flame. Frankly, she was surprised LA wasn't full of flaming rain puddles. From her vantage point, the city was always more real and more like a postapocalyptic movie.

The cigarette merely sizzled, shed a few glowing embers. But the man bent toward her.

"I have to say . . . that was a nice parallel park, little lady."

"Oh, gee, congratulations for noticing," she piped up.

At her hip, the lady, we'll call her Jill, carried a coil of leather with a tiny grappling hook. It glinted in the sun, blinded the man for a moment. He thought the small woman looked like the adventuress Lara Croft—a half-digital, half-analog version; then again, partly, curiously hologram. She was small enough to have stepped out of a game screen but her flesh was realish à la Angelina Jolie. She had realish vibrating flesh, not only like Lara's or Angelina's but like the delicate holographic image of Princess Leia, beamed out of R2-D2. And the man, we'll call him Phil, who had spent a good deal of his life watching movies, wanted to pick her up and hold her small vibrating body in his hand.

Jill checked to see that her grappling hook was secure—she used it to scale stairs and to hoist herself onto chairs and tables. Today she had an appointment with a well-known movie producer. She would have to navigate her way into the bar in front of which she'd parked her pickup truck; she'd have to heave herself up the entrance stairs, dodge flat and high heels, and dart past the bouncer. And she would do it. She was begrudgingly ready to risk life and limb—despite or maybe with the help of this man standing before her.

She paused and looked up at him. He was probably a regular. He had a goatee and messy shoulder-length hair, not merely meant to look unwashed but truly unwashed—for which she kind of liked him. He was very thin and wore thick Martin Scorsese glasses, heavy architecture on his fine-boned face. And he nurtured a drawn look; he had an inward curl to his body that suggested he thought himself too smart for LA but would probably keep living here anyway—advertising his disenchantment and being too sensitive for his surroundings.

Jill knew that once inside the bar she wouldn't need him anymore. She'd been to bars like this. Next to fish-thin waitstaff she would expand, not just to her normal size, but beyond.

"Do you know the owner, Mike Swanson?" the lady asked, pointing to the entrance of the bar—a door arched and scalloped like a seashell, and cut into a slab of white marble.

"Ha!" Phil replied. It was a response that denoted a relationship, but also a response she didn't want to indulge.

She quickly asked, "Will you show me inside?" She smiled up at him, with a slight buzz which signaled either attraction or a coming growth spurt.

Phil, for his part, was still awash in her resemblances: A miniature Linda Hamilton? GI Jane? Or, oops, his mother circa 1971? He felt at a loss, but came up with, "Are you sure you want to sell your soul?"

"Of course not," Jill said. "I want to write *and* direct."

Phil was confused.

The truth was, Jill had just moved to LA from Iowa with a singular and burning desire to make a movie about tragic merpeople. She'd envisioned a whole extended family. They walked around LA, squeezed into leather pants or fishnets, opalescent leggings, or pencil skirts—the kind of clothing that would remind their legs of their lost fishiness, or fusion. At around midnight in bars along the Sunset Strip, just as the merpeople were getting to know a potential someone, who might kiss them and reverse their exile on land, the skin behind their ears would start to itch. They'd run a finger along this secret pocket and feel a feathering of scales. And they'd know the scales would spread—first cropping up at their elbows and ankles, then crawling along their arms like growing patches of eczema. Sometimes the scales would fall off their bodies as they fled home to underground sleeping tanks. Potential lovers might try to trace a trail of scales, glowing translucent sequins that evaporated on a fingertip like a snowflake.

The man from the sidewalk extended his palm and the little lady hopped on. She took care to position one prong of her grappling hook securely around his middle finger and pull tightly on the coil of leather for leverage.

"Ouch," he said.

Jill: "Did I offend your sense of chivalry?"

Phil: "You hurt me. I'm bleeding."

"Shall I kiss it and make it better?"

And then Phil laughed. "You're funny!" he said.

And Jill said, "Imagine that."

The bouncer at the entrance to the bar had a walrus neck and a bald head that might have contained sonar, for without turning to see the pair approach he asked, "Back again so soon, Phil?"

"This little lady has an appointment with Mike," said Phil. But now that the bouncer faced them, he couldn't find Jill. A crowd of women, all glammed up, with flashing slabs of new white dental work, scurried up the steps. They were clutching small purses and batting superhuman eyelashes.

"What, where is she?" the bouncer asked, dazed and dazzled in the wake of the rushing women. Phil extended his hand and the walrus man squinted. Jill had the disappointing sensation of simultaneous expansion and dissolution; of slipping off Phil's hand and landing sturdily on the ground. She felt her fleshy borders slip and wiggle—she was untanned, not-so-sculpted, generally unenhanced. Luckily, Jill had remembered that morning to draw on her eyebrows. She raised one, like an inverted check mark, and leaned in so the walrus could find the focal point. He got it, stood back, and with very little enthusiasm filled the rest of her in.

He ushered the pair through a velvet-curtained door and down a curving tunnel that grew progressively darker until another curtain was pulled back and they were suddenly underwater. The little lady thought of her merpeople. Her heroine, Violet Fin, would feel at home here.

The bar walls were all aquarium, where fish made their slow and fast movements; glinting silver darters, flattened tropical varieties, slowly fluctuating. It was the aquatic equivalent of women on poles, swaying as if caught in the trance of the water. Even without the women, the dimly lit room held the promise of ease and return to the womb—to sleep and to nothing but the slow fading throb of your own heartbeat. This room was all about finishing, and she thought of all the famous deals that must have gone down here and made men big.

Yet her merpeople were not ambitious. Or, weren't they? She wasn't really sure about that yet. She knew they didn't want to live in fear of their bodies' changes, of being stuck somewhere far away from their sleeping tanks, say a taxi at 11:00 PM, just as the gills began to bud and open along their necks. But she also knew Violet didn't simply want to return to the safety of the ocean. She was half land girl now. She wanted to have the freedom to move between air and water breathing states at will. She wanted to be in charge of her body's shifting shapes and boundaries. Maybe it was a bit of a stretch, or even really ironic, to imagine that her merpeople could have these things by finding a person with whom to fall in love.

Jill imagined Violet sitting at the bar, ordering Diet Pepsi, anxiously waiting for someone to look at her with a gaze that neither clutched nor clung, a gaze that caressed and enhanced every freckle and fissure on her sun-dried skin. A gaze that wrapped her in a glowing halo and secretly intuited her fluidness of spirit; that saw in fine detail the complexity of who she wanted to be. Jill imagined Violet growing very impatient. She imagined Violet mid-conversation, saying, "Look, will you just kiss me already?"

She imagined that Violet, in lieu of the love cure, might seek out shadier options. Jill was only beginning to imagine what those might be.

Now, as Phil hooked his hand around Jill's elbow, she realized she'd grown. She was bigger than her baseline five feet three and a half inches, and along with the expansion of flesh came the increase in blood volume and the desire to fuck. Another good and bad consequence, depending on the circumstances, of her continually fluctuating size.

She turned on Phil, pulling away from his light clutch. "Don't think that because I let you carry me in your hand you can take liberties," she said, realizing how she was enjoying the dramatics of the rippling aquarium light.

Phil backed up and bared his palms. He hung his head so Jill had to bend her knees and cock her head to see his face shifting through different expressions, masking and muffling, until he popped up with a mostly disengaged, slightly amused smile.

"I'm not an egg baby, a fuzzy chick, or a small animal in need of rescue," Jill said to make sure he got the point—yet at the same time she checked out his shoulder-to-hip ratio.

"I guess I did want to tell you not to be afraid of the big man Mike," said Phil.

"I knew it," Jill said, as she looked at his lips and motioned for him to lead her on while she followed at a safe distance behind.

Phil turned and led Jill out of the room and down another white hallway. For his part, as he watched Jill stand in front of the flickering aquariums, he'd felt something come alive in him other than irony. Although there was that too. While Jill had been thinking about her merpeople Phil had been in the den, the dark den of his adolescence, learning how to be a man by watching Humphrey Bogart and Ingrid Bergman, with her shivering glycerin tears. Mike walked by the entrance to the den with his real live date, Melinda Fox, who pulled back, leaned sinuously into the room, and said, "Who's that?" and pointed to Phil who sat in a recliner with a bowl of freshly popped movie-night popcorn.

"Who's that?" Mike repeated, sticking his head into the den. He flipped on the overhead light to reveal Phil in his pajamas, which were patterned with miniature Scottie dogs.

"Oh, that's the king of the gaylords," said Mike. Phil, who'd just shoved a super-large handful of popcorn into his mouth, tried to smile.

Now, fifteen years later, he said, "A gay*lord* already is a king, you can't be a king of the gaylords, it's redundant, dumbass!"

"What?" asked Jill, the white hallway suddenly resembling a futuristic loony bin.

"Mike's my brother," Phil told Jill.

"OK."

"So without me he's nothing," said Phil, rather too desperately.

Phil wanted to tell Jill that Mike made his original money on cigar bars and paintball playgrounds—that Mike's true calling was discovering and capitalizing on macho bro-culture fads. He wanted to tell her that he, Phil, was the real film man—a connoisseur, an MFAster, a maker of movies himself. He had pointed Mike in the direction of several solidly written popcorn crunchers, from which Mike had made millions. He'd done it in exchange for funding for his own project, *Cries and Cries*. But if he said all of this, he would have to tell her that he made *Cries and Cries*, his sad masterpiece that no one had gone to see.

Now they approached another large arched door and for a moment Jill thought it was a rippling wall of water. It danced sinuously in the light with the pearlescent sheen of an ocean after an oil spill. As they moved closer the ripples stilled and Jill saw that the door was inlaid with the insides of abalone shells. She stopped and cupped her fingers along a shell as if to scoop up the ghost of its former inhabitant.

"Mike doesn't hunt these, does he?" she asked.

A smile moved across Phil's face. And something in Jill sunk like a diving bell.

She'd recently read an article about abalone hunters. The article had called the practice "the new most dangerous game," yet Jill had not felt bad about the northern California divers who lost their lives in pursuit of the elusive sea snails. These were hunters who dove with knives to cut through the thick ropes of seaweed, just as knights had fought their way through thickets like pubic hair, or scaled the skirts of castles to claim poor alabaster princesses, tender white mussels who, just like Greta Garbo, wanted to be left alone.

After reading the article, Jill went online and found a YouTube video in which a proud diver energetically shucked an abalone, then laid it out on a platter and prodded its organ sac for tiny, throwaway pearls. On the sidebar of her computer screen came hundreds of such videos, showing how to dice, fry, and season the delicacy—the videos multiplied like different varieties of porn.

Her mermaids would not like this.

Violet, a mostly good feminist and eco-critic, would not like it at all. There was something very awful and stupid, Jill thought, about choosing to hunt a creature that so resembled, in all its metaphorical configurations, a vagina.

She pushed open the heavy door.

Mike Swanson sat at the back of a large dark room cast into silhouette by a bright wall-sized fish tank behind him. At first he seemed to be asleep; his head slumped into his chest, his legs kicked up sideways onto a large desk. As Jill walked forward the room was quiet but for a click, click, click, too irregular for an aquarium pump or air conditioner. Yet the only things moving in the room were the fish, though barely. Drugged or bored they hung like puppets, flapping a flipper every now and then as if paid to do it.

As a girl Jill had thought there was something lonely about walking through Chicago's big indoor aquarium. She'd been surprised by the strange suspension of sound, being so close to all that flickering life yet not able to touch or hear anything. As she continued across the room the light from the fish display leaked around Mike's edges and divided along the shiny facets of his alligator cowboy boots, turning him into half menacing water creature.

Jill stood five feet away. She was close enough to see Mike's hands working what she thought was a cell phone but then realized was a small plastic hula dancer. Mike pressed his thumb into the base of her circular stand and she collapsed, not neatly with a bow or a bend in the knees as if to commence the hula, but in complete prostration—limbs and torso crumpling into a lump. When he released the button she popped back up as if nothing had happened—the past was erased. Her eyes bright, ruby lips just slightly, mockingly smiling. Mike pressed and released, pressed and released. He pressed, pressed, pressed, and seemed ready to fling the defective dancer when Jill wavered across his radar.

The lady now in front of Mike was large and flexible looking. Fully erect, she was at least six feet tall. She carried a shiny multipronged piece of metal equipment at her side. She was a late-night TV show warrior princess, a first masturbatory fantasy. It was Mike's birthday, and he thought, yes, this is more like it.

The hula dancer had been a gift from the walrus. It had been Mike's only gift in a long, disappointing day. But now his bros had come through for him. Though which bro was observant enough to understand what he liked, he didn't know or really want to think about. Whoever had sent her understood that he liked a challenge. A woman who might, theoretically, beat him up.

"Well, hello there," Mike said, straightening in his chair. He heard how his voice sounded canned, but this was role playing, right? Only Phil would accuse him of being permanently canned. Phil who had just quit. On his birthday. He'd actually said, "I'm just disappointed in the common moviegoing audience, you know, people." Mike, a.k.a. "the dumb one," had said, "Well, good luck avoiding them."

Jill watched as Mike raised his crossed legs, hovered them an inch above the table, and slowly lowered them to the floor in a not-so-subtle demonstration of abdominal strength. She began to worry more acutely about her mermaids. Violet would never find a human who really saw her, or could love her for her desire to be free. Mike Swanson didn't even recognize her. Granted, the other night at the party, she hadn't been quite so tall. But she'd talked to him for twenty minutes! She'd described the merpeople's outfits and he said, "So they'll be hot?"

She nodded her head yes, hesitantly. Her heroine Violet Fin would be sexy though not skinny: she'd have real thighs and a belly roll. Mike had given her his card.

And now Phil flicked on the overheads.

Mike blanched in the light, puckering his face. "What the fuck, Phil?"

"Just wanted to make sure you treat this little lady with respect," Phil said.

"Little lady?" was Mike's reply.

Jill looked down at her growing biceps—she was passing the seven-foot mark. She flexed her fingers, shifted her weight from one foot to the other to regain balance. Her self-perception hadn't caught up with the size of her body and this sometimes gave her vertigo. And she was annoyed. She hated that people didn't see things more clearly—she hated projections, and un-careful looking, but even more she hated fluorescent lighting—the way it left no room for the imagination.

The light shot down from buzzing tubes on the ceiling and Jill felt it as fine shards of fiberglass; inhalable, invisible, piercing the skin. It made the room much smaller and a hundred times uglier—revealing piles of boxes, and one wall only half-covered in mint-green paint. There was a dartboard on the wall, a leather couch set in front of a big-screen TV and a gaming console. There was a life-size cardboard cut-out bikini model holding a beer. There was the hazy flashback to the couple of times she'd been inside frat houses, and the all-around feeling of stunted growth.

"Are you really the Mike Swanson who produced *Cries and Cries*?" Jill asked.

Now it was Mike's turn to smile. "Funny that you bring that up," he said. "That was Phil's special project."

"Well, I liked it," said Jill.

"She liked it," said Phil affirmatively, and then he said, "You did?"

To be precise, Jill had liked some of *Cries and Cries*. As a whole the movie was pretentious, overly bloated with references, and in bad need of a new title. But there were beautiful moments. She liked the Bergmanesque close-ups that lingered so long, the young heroine's face became as indeterminate and strange as a word said over and over again. She liked that the movie was told from a girl's point of view, and she appreciated the nods to *Picnic at Hanging Rock* and *The Spirit of the Beehive*—movies about girls' metaphorical death at adolescence, though she wished that instead of death, those movies had been about transformation. Girls' spirits didn't really die when they entered the world of women versus men, dark versus light, passive versus active; their spirits often transmuted into something smarter, and stranger—less understood, but strong.

"Well," said Jill with a sigh, "I came because I admired you for making that movie." And then, "Got to go now!"

Mike said, "Wait!" He walked around his desk, filled his lungs with air, and spread his arms out—he went wide, since, next to Jill, he could no longer go tall. "Nobody went to see that film," Mike said with the same sly smile Jill had seen Phil use—though on Phil it looked like a disguise. "If nobody went to see that film, which you so admired, what makes you think anybody will go to see what you have? Ah yes, I remember, the little mermaids...?"

This sounded like equal parts insult and opening.

But Jill had already noticed something, and connected it to the door inlaid with abalone shells. It was Mike's soul, perhaps, hanging from a hook in the corner by the fish. It was the black suit of a scuba diver, headless and handless, and shimmering as if still wet.

"People will go to my movie because it'll be better," Jill called out, turning and heading to the door. Her fingers laced automatically around the leather coil of the grappling hook. Sometimes, when she was cresting the seven-foot mark, her body simply did things. Things for which she could not take responsibility.

Behind her she felt Mike's eyes, tracking.

Phil yelled out, "Can I call you?"

Outside Jill was no longer in danger of falling cigarettes or crushing drop ceilings. Her horizon line was a cluster of girls' heads flipping their flatironed hair up against metal and glass, and up above that, the oily human-made sunset.

She decided that her mermaids would prefer a smaller production company, and that anyway, she now had more to write. She saw a new option for Violet's freedom. The angry god who had banished her merfamily to land would surely accept a human sacrifice as reparation. She wondered if the flesh of a human would taste as succulent as the flesh of an abalone. The flesh of a human who had violated the laws of the sea.

Dora

The first time Dora came back I didn't recognize her.

She appeared at our party as a ripple in the wallpaper, as an outline of a young woman whose cloak matched the damask—her hair, a mess as usual, was now a hovering arrangement of funeral flowers.

Our father had died only a month before, and I was busy with his friends, high-ranking party officials who had come about the money. Today these men were sheet metal. Only their eyes were alive, wide and trapped in steel casing. I was sure any grief they had over my father's passing escaped their bodies in toxic fumes.

So my eyes wandered as I talked. Flitted out and around the men's dull heads, and I caught glimpses of her—moving to sit on the high-backed sofa, though, here, her face blurred and her skin absorbed the ripples in the silk. I saw her walk across the Oriental carpet, its swirls and arabesques curled up around her legs like vines. It wasn't until she passed by a window that I understood that her body was delineated by tiny holes, empty cells, like pin perforations made in paper, and that those holes shifted inside her to absorb the shape or pattern of whatever she stood in front of. There in the window the sun shone right through her. She was a woman-shaped tree—strings of tiny lights wrapped intricately around her branches. She was just as I imagine she always wanted to be.

Perhaps it was my father's death that made her appearance possible. For the last month everything had seemed like a photographic illusion, a double-exposed photograph in which the two takes almost, but don't quite, match. In one take my father was still alive; in the second my father had died too early, without, I felt, ever really knowing me.

As soon as I could escape the friends I climbed the stairs to my old perch in a corner of the second-story balcony where Dora and I used to crouch and peer through the balustrade, eavesdropping on parties like this. Above me rose the suit of armor, seventeenth-century and mottled, arms sealed at its sides. When I was a boy I dreamt I was trapped inside it, vanished to oblivion inside my own home. Sometimes I'd dream my father was trapped in an identical suit, and we stood in silence, our voices stolen, in much the same way we sat for Sunday dinner.

The sun was setting and the chandeliers had not been lit. In the large foyer she was nearly invisible. She hovered and listened over shoulders yet took care never to betray herself, never to stay in one place for too long. When she stopped for one, two, three seconds her cells clumped together, the perforations clustered into vaguely familiar features.

But I stopped myself. I was a painter of portraits. How many sketches had I made in which the subject resembled me, or her; in which my yearning made the models grow long noses, and close-set eyes?

And then I lost track of her. I didn't notice the ripple on the stairs until she was three or four steps up, heading toward me. I pressed back against the wall and listened to the tap of her feet, accompanied by a third beat, which I first imagined came from the tip of an umbrella. But the sound was too pronounced for an umbrella; it was more like the sound of a gavel or a wooden walking stick tipped in steel. It was an announcement of presence. And then the sound stopped. Her steps proceeded softly to the center of the balcony. And then stopped again.

I knew I should move. Discover her. I was a grown man, famous in certain circles, inheritor of the estate. I was a painter of portraits; men and women sat for me until I uncovered their secrets. I revealed people to themselves and they thanked me for it, though not, I think, my father. He sat for me once, many years after Dora left, and when he looked at the finished portrait his face sealed into its final defensive mask. "Is that how you see me?" he asked.

I stepped out toward her; she had her back to me and was leaning against the banister and looking out over it. With my step she grew more solid. She turned and revealed herself, for the game was on her terms.

Dora wore the unfashionable thick wool cloak she had left in, and her hair was loose and by now streaked with a silvery gray. She held a rifle in her left hand, her rifle for shooting birds, her most unwomanly rifle. It was the beat I'd heard on the stairs.

When I reached her side I too looked out over the party, at all my father's foreshortened and black-suited friends.

"Should I shoot them?" she asked with a smile in her voice.

And I said, "No, Dora. They're just birds."

But I didn't dare move. I had found her again, my wild and prodigal twin. And I needed her to stay there, poised and by my side.

Winona

1.

Winona wakes up on a pillowcase that hasn't been changed in a year. She secretly likes the smell of it. Likes to fall asleep to her scent, and then linger in the morning, a few moments with it, as with an illicit lover. She is half awake, and half lying on the porch of her grandmother's old colonial in Georgia. She's lying in a crooked shape, as if she's doing the Charleston on her back, but really she's been stabbed in the gut. A black-handled cheese knife sticks out of her stomach and a glass of iced tea balances on her chest. She's concentrating on the iced tea glass, which is rising and falling with her breath—if she moves to pull out the knife the tea will spill and pool between her hip bones, run down between her legs, saturate and ruin the watered silk of her best Sunday dress. The smell of sweaty hair floats into the dream along with something more sour—matted fur or rotting fall leaves. Sugar drifts down through her glass, and melts at the bottom like sticky snow.

It's hot on the dream porch, but it's hotter in her bedroom, and she doesn't want to wake up. She wants to hurry up and die in the dream—she thinks that rather than leaving, she'll finally join her body, be one with the sweat, blood, and sugar, and she has to get there before her mother knocks on her bedroom door, or walks out on the porch and notices one of several things: the ring of iced-tea perspiration gathering on her dress, her deathlike stillness, the missing cheese knife.

At this time of the morning Winona can often control her dreams. She falls into them like falling into a stage set, but once inside can walk around, pick up and move objects. She has freedom because she hasn't been trained in the customs of each dream world; each one is different and ready to read, by only her. This is the way she felt when she was really acting. Even if she was only an extra, swaying, trancelike, in the background of her high school's musical theater productions.

But today the mother is there too, and the setting is partly Tennessee Williams, partly the same old Kansas City, Kansas.

She hears the heels of her mother's shoes clacking not along wood porch, but cold kitchen tile. She tries to melt them with her dream powers, sees them puddle and smoke, deflate and shrivel like the wicked witch's feet in that scene from *The Wizard of Oz*.

"Oh," she says out loud, puncturing the air. She is hurting her mother. She's awake—and there is the knock. It makes her jump and the little dog too, her little Toto, who sleeps at the foot of her bed and is dying of cancer. He falls and lands on the ground with a thump.

"Dear, are you up?" her mother asks, her voice splintering wood. She looks down at the dog—for a moment she hopes he's finally dead.

"Yes," she says, short and clipped.

"Don't forget Riley's pills," her mother says in her irritating Doris Day–like way, the way Doris would talk to someone below her. Not unkind but firm, with an unconscious easy power, an overabundance of capability. The heels click away, recede, and Winona bends down toward Riley. She scrapes her fingers around his oily belly, lifts him, kisses his forehead, the only place he doesn't smell of matted fur, rotted leaves, and medication. She puts him back on the bed. Riley is dreaming of nothing.

Winona moves into the bathroom. She doesn't look at her face in the mirror except in furtive glances, as if someone else were in the room—a presence partly her mother, partly her father, partly her church, and partly the psycho killer from American movies who kills the vain girls first.

Instead, she practices what may be artistic minimalism. She has rules for herself. She'll not brush her hair out fully, just a few strokes to keep in most of the frizz, and no makeup. Doesn't think she needs deodorant—doesn't smell her armpits to find out. She'll brush her teeth, try hard to make it to twenty strokes, pee, wipe, but won't flush—it wastes water, and she's heard something about the dye on the daintily printed toilet paper her mother buys, something bad it does to the environment—although she's not sure what that is.

When she finishes non-cleansing, she allows herself to look in the mirror. The mirror, after all, is a beautiful antique from her mother's side of the family, so old it's almost human. It was her grandmother's, then her mother's. Spots of rust bloom up to the surface like sprigs of bloody baby's breath, and sometimes her reflection looks blurred, as if the mirror has taken a deep breath and stretched her out along its surface.

Recently Winona glued wampum beads around the carved coils and gold leaf of the mirror. She did this in rebellion against her mother who laughed when Winona asked if the family had secret Native American lineage. She said, "We gave you a Native American name because we were hippies, darling." And Winona, who had lately felt a quickening anger, and a desire to direct it toward something specific and culturally agreed upon, felt a part of that anger, a shard, an arrowhead, break apart and lodge itself in her mother's side.

Today Winona, the firstborn, places her head amid the speckles of blood and becomes a martyred saint. This year, her junior year of high school, she's switched her fascination from Joan of Arc, to "Princess" Aracoma of the Shawnee, to Greta Garbo. Garbo may not have been a saint but she was definitely a martyr. A woman who lent her body to America and let them partially, but not completely, remake it into their version of beautiful.

Sometimes Winona will look at the pictures of Garbo in a book she borrowed from the drama department. She'll wonder if Garbo was ever able to enjoy her beauty, or if it was always work, along with the anxiety of losing it and getting older like her grandmother—a real wicked witch, who has had so many plastic surgeries she'll stick to the bottom of the incinerator if she's ever finally cremated.

She sits on the toilet and flips through her book. Looking at certain pictures, she feels a frightening and exciting rush of recognition. There's something about the arch of Garbo's eyebrow, or the long thin nose, that she sees in herself. It's hard to tell about the eyes. Garbo's eyes were always elsewhere, heavy lidded and obscured by those curling eyelashes.

Lately Winona forgets that she has chosen not to be beautiful, that it's dangerous to be looked at too much—by Milo, her younger brother, by men at the gas station. Sometimes she forgets her theory that Garbo ran away because she was evaporating, changing to semi-solid water and then to air from all those looks. Her physics teacher has told her that molecules change shape when they're observed, and although she seems outwardly aloof, even a little rigid like her mother, she is secretly very soft inside.

Riley heaves in the bedroom. Winona tries to visualize the tumors inside him, change them into the sharp smooth crystals growing in the dark of a geode before it's cracked open. She hates to extend Riley's death with painkillers, to put two kinds of killers into his body.

But her mother says, "A drugged dog is a happy dog."

A drugged dog is like the drugged grandmother, Winona thinks, hooked up to tubes in the fancy nursing home—a drugged dog does not have to be dealt with. Her mother thinks she's doing her a favor by letting Riley live on in her care, and the more Winona lets her think this the more it becomes true.

Winona observes Riley in a concentrated way. She focuses down to the molecules. She observes that he's dreaming now, dreaming of fast-motion films, of flowers blooming and decaying and blooming again.

2.

In the kitchen Winona's mother Franny has forgotten there is a dying dog and a dying grandmother, but she hasn't forgotten, exactly. She remembers everything with her body—the dog, and her mother's judgments. She carries them physically, in edema, an extra layer of water that makes her always feel slightly off, displaced, like a figure that's been erased and redrawn, half an inch to the left. Lately she's been feeling that the displacement not only keeps her from her better self, but that it keeps her from Winona, who is drifting away from her, who has lovely and dangerous new friends.

She works her way through the kitchen, stiff and tall, with crisp jerky movements to compensate for her lack of place. Her hair rests in a neat silver bowl, with razored edges, over her head. She's never been comfortable in the kitchen. She had maids when she was growing up, the counters were high, white, and pristine, and when she entered through the swinging doors she felt she was trespassing into someone else's space. Here, her kitchen feels miniature, pretend, and inadequate, and she doesn't know what to do with the ugly metal knobs of the sink. The water is running, but she forgets how to turn it off—she turns one knob to the left and scalding water shoots out. She turns the other handle and the water gets hotter. Her hands are following the wrong pattern. Is it the one from the master bathroom? She's lived in this house for fifteen years. She has run it, and suddenly she forgets.

Today, in this kitchen, she has to be careful about the way she sets the coffee down on the table in front of her husband and son because she cannot seem to make the contact between the mug and the counter soft and loving. She tries this morning and her hand shakes, hovers an inch above the table, and hot coffee splashes onto her skin.

"Oh, honey," her husband says.

"Oh, Mom," her son Milo says, always trying to gain points by imitating his dad. Milo jumps up to hug her with his chubby body, so stupidly good-natured and unrestrained. It comes from her husband's side of the family, she thinks—that wild openness of underbreeding which was so charming in her husband when they first met, back when they were hippies and it was a political statement. Now she sees that this friendly exuberance allows both father and son to get away with not seeing her enough to know how to really help.

For example, despite Milo's hug, her hand is still covered in coffee; neither of them offers her a napkin. Norm has returned to his newspaper, benevolently oblivious. Useless, Franny thinks. But then there is Winona.

Winona appears at the kitchen door, takes a rag, and wipes the table where her mom has spilled. Winona! her mother sighs—she is her disheveled angel. Winona is the only one who understands her silent demands, and won't make her say things out loud. But when Winona gives the rag to her mother, she doesn't wipe her hand.

She says, "Here, Mom," but tenderly and as if in apology.

Franny has noticed, has tried not to, but here it is again: Winona will not touch or come close to her, unless she does so first. Still, a bit of her has relaxed from Milo's hug, as if the pressure inside her body were not water, but air, as if a little bit of air has been released and transferred to him, making him even fatter.

Pshhhhh.

Winona moves into the kitchen, turns on the tap. Franny is stuck again; she has stepped into a puddle of thinking. She has come to the point where she thinks, it's not fair, she didn't intend to become the ruler of the house and she didn't intend to pass this burden on to Winona, who is already at work cleaning the breakfast dishes.

In the beginning, the managing of lives was a joy to her, a challenge, a way to prove that she wasn't a spoiled rich girl—that she could care for her children without the help of nannies and servants. But there was always more to do, things that Norm could never see, and these things multiplied and she kept lists of them in her journal, which she left open on the nightstand, so that Norm might catch a glimpse and decide to participate. There was her part-time job outside the house, and the way she felt herself at the center of a web on which their lives hung like little trembling dewdrops, vulnerable, always about to grow too heavy at the bottom, to slip, to flood out of her control. She had to cook the right food, schedule the right doctor's appointments, and make sure each child progressed morally, physically, and steadily through multiplying stages of life.

For Winona there was Bluebirds, Girl Scouts, Junior Assembly, and Cotillion. There was track or swim team every year, acting in church productions, participation in youth groups and church activities. For high school, she knew Winona should take at least two years of Spanish, physics, and calculus, all honors classes, belong to several student organizations such as Students Against Drunk Driving, and volunteer in the community, in order to be accepted into the small private and exclusive New England college where she had met Norm. But it's not as if she's controlling. Winona can do whatever else she chooses, when she has the time. And even though she's nervous about Winona's interest in theater, it's not as if she is trying to erase Winona's individuality. She knows and loves Winona's weaknesses: her pigeon-toed walk, her lack of coordination, her concentrated look of putting too much effort into moving, her thick ankles and calves. Secretly, she likes Winona's flaws because they echo the flaws in herself. They're imprints and marks of ownership. They are also secrets they share that can be used against her.

For example, last week when Winona arrived home late from an outing with Angela, Franny asked about her day and noticed how

Winona said all the right things, in a list, all the things Franny already knew, in that crisp manner, so much like her own that it felt like mocking. So as Winona walked away she offered something more intimate, said, "I'm sorry you inherited those thick calves from me," and Winona, who always wore long flared pants in an attempt to disguise her ankles, stopped as if taking a blow to the stomach, and walked quickly out of the kitchen.

Yes, Franny can see it now—she is what some people would call a bitch. She is the reason the family does most of what it does and the reason they don't do it very enthusiastically.

And now she's breathing faster as Winona's new friend Angela pulls into the driveway. She can hear her music, "ba boom, ba boom boom," from the breakfast table. Winona quickly looks up at her. "Angela's picking me up so we can study after school."

Franny is suspicious—Winona usually tells her these things further in advance.

Norm, who hears only half of what is said, is suddenly alert and serious. He says, "You're not going in my car," because his cars are his love affairs: shiny, voluptuous, and guarded. Because Franny and Winona drive his cars, which he repairs and later will sell, he makes them mark down the gas mileage on grid paper every time they go out, and he believes that because of his system they drive no farther than is necessary. Franny notices Winona stiffen at Norm's remark and knows she's been slipping out of the grid. Norm, of course, doesn't suspect this, Franny thinks. He has very little imagination.

"Hello, new friend," Norm says as Angela comes through the door, and, jolly and detached, he goes back to his toast. Franny shoots darts into Norm's soft flesh. Now she must be friendly too.

She looks at Angela, with her bumper-sticker-covered backpack and safety-pin earrings. She says, "Well, you girls are just so avant-garde," and reminds herself that friends are another item on her list of things that Winona should have.

As Angela saunters into the living room and sits on the couch, Franny is watching. She watches from the kitchen as Angela eyes her eclectic but expensive arrangement of knickknacks on the coffee table—a mix of Native American artifacts and Victorian-era antiques. She picks up a glass paperweight and places it on top of a tintype photograph of a Shawnee woman so the woman's face is suddenly stretched and magnified, haloed by the colored butterflies in the glass. Angela leans back and looks at it, satisfied. Franny, who is proud of her decorations, which are much more artistic and liberal minded than those of other mothers, has noticed that every time Angela leaves a room something is changed—a vase is turned upside down, dried flowers are poked behind picture frames. Franny is afraid that Angela is making a comment on her lack of whimsy. So as Angela steps into the kitchen, she catches her.

"You know, Angela," she says, "I think you must be a genius." Franny puts her hands on Angela's shoulders, smiles triumphantly and ironically, and says, "Yes, Angela, a genius." Angela looks startled, but manages an "OK, Franny, sure."

Franny regrets it—it was a bad move. Is she so pathetic that she has to resort to intimidating teenagers? And it's not that she lacks whimsy or spontaneity; it's just that her whimsy has changed. When she was younger she was like Angela, she thought spontaneity existed in the moments when a true self flashed through all the undeniable false stuff, made a question mark out of peas at a stuffy dinner party like George Emerson in that Forster novel (or was that the movie?). Now her moments of spontaneity involve the false stuff. Now, her spontaneity requires analysis.

There was the other day. She had asked Norm to take out the trash, and when he did it without complaining, and the bag split and the trash spilled all over the yard, she laughed loud, hard, spontaneous laughter. Was she pleased that he was unsuccessful? Pleased to have proof that she was the one who kept things running? Norm had looked sad. Had put on his I'm-too-helpless-to-help look. His I-have-a-heart-condition look.

Bitch, she thinks. Perhaps it serves her right that Norm is the one the children look to for fun, to goof off with, even if it's just to reassure them that he is not going to die.

She hears the front door open and calls out to Winona, to catch her before she leaves, and her voice is too urgent.

"Did you give Riley his medicine?" Franny asks.

"Yes," Winona says with a tinge of annoyance, and the usual two pecks, one on each cheek. But Franny can't rest—she follows the girls to the door and notices Winona's hair. She'll only comb it out halfway, and the frizziness, this unkemptness, her loose men's shirt and baggy cotton pants, make her look odd, unsettling, vaguely sexy. She reaches out and puts a hand on either side of Winona's head, and Winona freezes.

She says, "Oh, honey, you'd look so much more attractive with hot rollers." Winona stands perfectly still, as if concentrating. Angela looks at Franny over Winona's shoulder, shakes her head, and smirks.

3.

Today Winona is getting a tattoo after school with Angela. Angela's tattoo will go all the way around her upper arm. Winona's will be a shooting star that will hide at the base of her hip bone, barely an excuse for a tattoo—from a distance it will look like the shadow of a scar.

Inside the tattoo parlor the walls are full of art, dragons with blood-red eyes, hundreds of bare-breasted women floating on miens of their own hair, skulls, and motorcycles. As she lies down on the padded dentist's chair, her eyes catch on the word "Mom," inscribed in a heart, and she quickly closes them and tries not to feel the small twinge of disgust for what she's doing, the same twinge that makes her close off her body when her mother is around, or when she finds herself looking at the backs of her mother's knees—a bas-relief of raised streaks of blue—or at the hard ridge from her nostril to the corner of her mouth like a brace holding it down. Her mother has not gotten soft and loose like other mothers, but too hard.

The tattoo artist opens two fingers and presses them down on the spot at her hip. Then he puts a finger on the space in between his fingers. He's an ordinary boy with dyed black hair, but he's exotic and sexy to Winona, and she's afraid that she could too easily fall in love.

The boy says, "You picked a good spot. I can feel your pulse right here." And Winona thinks of her other grandmother, not the one made of plastic but the one who was fast and loose, and now is soft and insane. For a second she appears in a bubble like the good witch, glossy and in the full bloom of her beauty.

She says, "Be where you are, Winona!" and vanishes.

The boy holds the electric needle in his hand and the moment before it touches her skin he says, "Breathe." All the softness in the world floods into that small space before the sting, shivers and hovers around the room in the dragon's wings, in women's breasts, in the silver electric hum of the needle.

4.

Franny has not wanted to have sex with Norm for a year now, but she does anyway. He pinches her while she's cooking and puts wet lips on the inside of her neck. She says, "Norm," and is suddenly angry. The children could be watching and she doesn't like the way he always draws attention to the rigidness of her body, or the way she has to tell him, "No," and, "Sit," like a dog, and the way he so easily obeys. Tonight after the kiss he slinks back to the couch, winks, and whispers, "Firecracker" to Milo who has already begun to construct an image of his ideal woman. She will be proud and stiff like his mother and Winona, and will wear shirts with crisp sleeves, and swishy long peasant skirts and pants that never say sex, only hint at it in their exotic patterns and loose movements.

Tonight, after he kisses her, Norm sits with the two children, watching reruns of *Saturday Night Live*, their favorite show. Franny doesn't find grown people imitating other grown people funny. Tonight they're laughing at the family of coneheads. Franny finds the coneheads' nasally voices and robotic movements both familiar and offensive—but as she passes through the living room, she tries out a laugh anyway. "Ha! Ha! Ha!" They look up, startled. She steps outside her laugh and hears it, and she is startled too.

She doesn't know how it happened. This stiffness. This horrible laugh. When she was young, she thought she was in her body—she had her passionate stories, *Jane Eyre* and *Wuthering Heights*. She fell in love not with the difficult, cruel men, but with the heroines, wild and fighting against their personal oppressions. She wore her hair long and stormy, and smoked cigarettes. But what was there to be angry about, really? Her mother told her it was absurd to be angry when you had money—it was even in poor taste.

But she is angry. She's angry with Norm, who sits on the couch comfortably with the children and comfortable in his body despite its folds and creases. She hates that Norm, like a child, or a biology teacher, is able to see his body as amazing. It's fascinating to him how the aspirin, nitroglycerin, and beta-blockers, three small pills, support and oil his miraculous machine of blood, electricity, and oxygen. Franny knows Norm loves her when she administers his pills in a Dixie cup, like a nurse—setting it down on his bedside table. She knows that as a young man Norm didn't think he would live past twenty-five—the age at which his father died. She knows that ever since boyhood he's held his breath while passing cemeteries in order to gain extra years. He has tricks for outsmarting death; he has faith in Franny, and modern medicine.

Franny is not sure she believes in herself, or modern medicine. There was the young surgeon who advised her to get rid of two olive-sized growths in her left breast. He said the fibrous growths were not cancerous, would not likely increase the chances of cancer later on, but if left unchecked, in some women, grew to the size of tennis balls. He gestured excitedly when he said this; with his fingers he made a circle the size of a grapefruit. Her operation left her with a smaller left breast and a white moon-shaped scar around her nipple. And last month, at a routine mammogram, the nurse who struggled to fit Franny's tiny breast between the machine's cold plates, listened to Franny's story and was startled. Fibrous tissue was simply fibrous tissue, she scolded. Some women had it and some did not. She mumbled something about surgeons, overzealousness, and the cutting up of perfectly healthy women.

Franny drove home from the mammogram remembering the two days coming out of anesthesia, trying to find her body under the bandages, hearing her heart beat strangely like she was listening underwater, like it was someone else's, someone right beside her.

And besides the surgery, Franny feels she now has to manage her body in ways she didn't have to before. New parts are forming and dividing where there was once one smooth surface. Now her cheeks form triangles like the tips of arrows pointing down, and she buys not one face cream but a separate eye cream, and an intensive repair serum for night. When she remembers to look at her body as a whole and from a distance she's surprised to find a tall attractive woman. It's a habit now to look at her body in sections, to take it apart.

As she gets ready for bed, Norm shuffles into the room. He sits on the edge of the bed contented with the meal that he was served, the fat-free pudding for dessert, and from laughing hard and through his belly with his children. He touches the leg of her cotton pajama pants, and his body, porous and folding, softens and blends into the bedsheets, into the blended smell of himself and her.

Franny feels all her edges pushing up and rubbing together. She remembers an exhibit of Picasso paintings she once saw, the weeping women. As Picasso got older his women multiplied into more and more cubes, grew fangs, and became monsters. She thought this was a result of Picasso growing old and mean and not getting any sex. She still thinks this, but she thinks too that the women had truly begun to feel like monsters, fractured and jagged. Tonight she'll not be able to close her eyes and enter into her favorite fantasy, that she's Catherine Deneuve in *Belle de Jour* and Norm is a paying customer. She rolls away and doesn't let him rub her leg until he becomes an anonymous man, until her eyes glaze over and she's in a hotel room. Tonight he is Norm, and she is a wicked weeping woman. She can't shake the feeling that he, in his simple happiness, in his not seeing her sadness, has betrayed her.

5.

Winona covers her tattoo for two weeks. Then it turns to hot summer weather, and she uses a Band-Aid. Out by the swimming pool Milo marches in with his gaggle of boys—outside of the house Milo is, surprisingly, a leader. The boys wear neckties, no shirts, and sombreros. They pick flowers from people's lawns, ring their doorbells, and serenade them with original songs and a bundle of their own uprooted flowers. Today, a woman yelled at Milo for picking her tulips, which would now die, very quickly, inside her house.

Milo is the true extrovert in the family, and to counter the jealous shaking of the family's heads at his social outings and faux pas, and to hide his real nervousness, he acts even more extroverted and absurd than he is. He plays himself, so that their judgment will soften to laughter.

Milo carries a wilted tulip for Winona, and when his friends have left he is struck by the sight of her. He lies down next to her in the deck chair at the edge of the pool, puts his arms to his sides, and kisses her cheek. She doesn't move because she likes his attention—he releases pressure in her body she didn't know she had.

Pshhhhh.

She kisses him back, and remembers not to laugh at him. She doesn't need to laugh anyway, now that the pressure is gone. Sometimes, although not today, she's uncomfortable with Milo's exuberantly physical attention. And it's true that Milo has recently started to notice his sister's body, its shadings and light, her armpit stubble, belly button. He sneaks touches of these places one by one, instead of pressing his whole body against hers as he used to in an innocent nonparticular hug. Now, he looks down at the shadow between her thighs and the slight rise up over it. What is underneath is not like the pictures in his friends' magazines, but innocent, like a pile of leaves that might smell damp and sweet, like rolling around in soft dirt under a honeysuckle bush at his grandmother's house.

He knows that Winona is too good to really be an object of desire, only bad women are sexual objects—although it's confusing because her breasts are full and so are her lips, and her teeth are large and white like polished stones. Still, Winona keeps her mouth closed, not parted, and looks at things sharply, and often out of the corner of her eye. She's the best one in the family, the only one his mother will let help in the kitchen, and she is the protector of Riley, the guider of his passage into death. Riley will not move from her bed, even though Milo and Riley used to be best friends.

Today Winona hugs Milo, kisses his forehead, and suddenly thinks of the boy. She sits up and says, "I want to show you something, but you have to keep it a secret." It's only a tiny star, she thinks. And lately she's felt beautiful and like sharing; lately she has been channeling not Garbo full of sadness, but Garbo full of light and humor. Sitting at the bus stop, she put down her book, swung her legs, and tilted her head up at the sky. She made a perfect stranger smile, someone she hadn't felt looking, a man with a deep resonant laugh. And there is the boy in her church choir who she stands beside, who has a creamy baritone voice. They went to Mexico together to help build a church with her youth group—she sees flashes of his tanned hands lifting white blocks of stone. She imagines there is something holy and purposeful about her attraction. Could they move to Mexico and adopt Mexican children? Could she be like Georgia O'Keeffe, and paint pictures of the bleached bones of seagulls that lie along the shore? She could get another tattoo, one of the boy's fingerprint, a copy of the time he touched her on the inside of her elbow.

She peels back the Band-Aid at her hip, but as she bends over Milo catches sight of the pink ring of her nipple peeking out from her bathing suit. He also sees the tattoo but isn't sure which one she's showing him. The two overlay in his mind so the shooting star turns into a vine inching over her breast, circling it, copying a photograph of a naked woman from one of his friends' magazines. This woman's tattoo ran all the way across her stomach, down to her vagina, which was shaved bare. Milo had wondered if she used the pink stuff that he'd seen Winona use on her legs to dissolve her hair—he'd tried it once on his own pubic hair when it came in only a year ago, but could only remove a couple of strands. Now his body gets confused, his pulse quickens.

Winona turns and looks at his erection. She gets up off the lounge chair slowly, as if it's a rattlesnake, so as not to make any sudden moves. Milo screams and swats at it.

"Oh, Milo," Winona moans. "Please pay better attention to your body." She turns and walks to the house and leaves him alone on the deck chair.

6.

During the summer Norm finally has time to work in the garage on his newest car. An activity more leisurely, but no less absorbing, than teaching high school biology. He likes to remind his family that his expert work at the old auto body shop helped support his mother, after his father died. Now he can finally buy his own broken-down cars, classy and rare models. He keeps the cars in his garage where no one is allowed without permission. He not only repairs all parts and does electrical and body work—he polishes and pampers the cars, smooths the leather seats with the best oil. Norm has told no one that with his newest car he'll attempt to master the flame job! The most delicate art of setting fire to metal—masking off the slick red and orange paint, so it curves with convincing felicity around the fender and fin. He has rented an air compressor, and a delicate metal airbrushing instrument he must hold in his hand like a lady's pistol. His plan is to surprise his family. He knows they think of him as distinctly unartistic.

It really isn't so. When he opens the hoods of his cars their shiny insides remind him of fine things—jewelry boxes, clockwork, human bodies. Cars are full of delicacies and complexities that he can fix, restore, get to purring. He's never told Franny that he set his sights on her because she reminded him of a white Firebird, long and lean and Grace Kelly–like. Virtuous, strong boned, and well bred—not too exotic, but definitely regal. When he was small a connection formed in his brain—he thought that his family's being poor was related to their poor health. His father died young, and his own eyesight went bad at age twelve. His love for Franny is real love but it's also a love that has lifted him up and strengthened the gene pool of his children. He thinks of them all in a row, tall, with smooth flesh and bright eyes—he fits in that row now too. Franny, he reminds himself, was a good investment. She may master him day by day, but over the long haul, she will have served him well.

7.

It's Milo who, coming back from a late-night romp around the neighborhood, sees Winona and the boy in the hot tub, after her parents have gone to sleep. Winona has looked in her mirror tonight, and on nights preceding this night, because she thinks she's changing into someone else. It's as if all her discipline and denial, her not looking in the mirror, washing her face, flushing, or combing her hair, has given rise to its opposite effect—to someone who is beautiful. She's allowing herself to accept this person, to be curious and playful with her, to comb her hair out fully.

Her hair is dark and rising, filled and curling with humidity, and her skin is moon-pale but plumped up with the moisture from the swimming pool. Her body prepared for this arrival by making an unexpected trip to Walgreen's for a *Wet and Wild*, ninety-nine-cent lipstick, a detour she wrote down as a field trip for her photography class in her father's mileage book. Now she colors her lips in like an actress in a play and walks out to the deck and sits with the boy on the top step of the swimming pool where the water laps up along the bottom edges of their bathing suits. Angela has just left with her boyfriend Arturo and Winona thinks they are probably having sex in the backseat of one of her father's cars, probably the one parked under her parents' bedroom window. This would normally worry her, but not here in her space of half dream, with freedom from judgment, where the dream seems to be mostly in control.

She thinks of Angela, how the wet strands of her hair dangled down to her breasts, how they left the boys in the hot tub and wandered off to the bathroom. She sat on the counter while Angela peed, and Winona asked her if she'd had sex with Arturo. Angela stood up without directly answering the question, and read Winona's mind. She said, "Do you think your choir boy would do it?"

Sometimes Winona objects to Angela's always getting at what she really wants to say, which in her family is considered rude. But tonight she says, "He might." For advice, Angela stands in front of Winona and pulls down the top of her bathing suit. She laughs and says, "Show him your tits." Winona fights off a gasp; Angela's are beautiful—full as the base of a teardrop, and with the large dark nipples Winona imagined a woman only achieved as an adult.

Now, sitting in the pool, Winona thinks this is surely a boy she *could* marry—if it ever came to that. He's kind and gentle, a little nervous. And didn't her mom sit on her bed, crisp and ironed for a serious talk, and much to Winona's horror pull condoms from her pocket and ask her if she knew what they were used for? When Winona said yes, her mother had said, surprisingly, "I would prefer you wait for marriage like I did, but I know things happen."

Out by the pool the boy puts his arm around Winona's shoulder, and she moves it to her knee. She wants to know what it feels like to have an orgasm. She's come close, touching around that place in bed, but then there is Riley, who every now and then lets out an annoyed squeak, as if to remind her to be respectful of the dying. And once she thinks of that, there are noises outside her door: her mother or brother who always want to know what she's doing. There are too many presences and needs in this house. Too many presences for which she feels responsible.

With her legs submerged in water, she knows the night air will soon get chilly. She has decided that in the world of a martyred saint, there are only brief windows for pleasure, so she moves the boy's hand up to the cotton crotch of her bathing suit, and it sits there motionless.

"Come on," she says. "We're not going to have sex." But when he asks, "Can I kiss you?" she says nothing. Kissing takes more skill than rubbing, and the last time they kissed it was too wet. She wants to hurry things up so she pulls down the top of her bathing suit, as Angela did. She moves out of herself again. She likes how her nipples look darker and soft in the moonlight, but is annoyed that the boy can barely touch them. His hands hover; they hover like her mother and brother. She rolls the bottom of her bathing suit down and twists it off, takes his hand and moves his fingers for him; she presses his middle finger into her, and thinks she can do it, split open, like a geode—she feels the little pinpricks like crystals all along her butt, running down the backs of her thighs. She lets the boy rub on his own now, looks up at the sky, but she can't slip away from him. She knows he's worried, there's something mechanical about the way his hand moves, too careful—she knows he doesn't want to be doing it but does it anyway. And this is when Milo steps on the dog toy in the bushes.

It lets out a long spindly squeak, the sound of pressure being released through a tiny hole.

Pshhhhh.

The boy jumps back and Winona pulls on her bathing suit. "I'm going in now," she tells the boy. She doesn't offer to walk him to his car and as she tries to dress she puts her leg through the wrong hole of her bathing suit so one butt cheek is exposed. She walks backward to the house. When she gets to the back door the boy is still standing there under the sycamore. She yells at him, "Leave!"

8.

In the house, quietly, Franny is dreaming of Catherine Deneuve. A whip cracks. Milo is shivery inside. Wrapped in the cocoon of his bedcovers he thinks Winona is the only girl he has ever loved, and she may be the only one who will ever love him back in his chubby body. Everybody loves Milo in general, it's common knowledge, but nobody loves Milo in a specific way. He doesn't fit in the special circle of intensity in which his mother loves Winona, carved in stone like a saint; his father loves his mother, like a Grace Kelly; and Winona loves her father, perhaps by default—because he's the only one who will conduct his business while she's around, who has business that is more engrossing than she is. But Milo loves Winona without being specially loved back. He is hers, she needs him, she just doesn't know it yet.

He thinks of how happy they are when they sit together on the sofa, how it is *he* who makes her laugh. Yes, she laughs at their dad too, but never because he's tried to make her laugh. Norm laughs at the TV and mostly at the same jokes—stuff like John Belushi crushing a can on his head, and anything that involves a fat man falling down. Milo tries to make her laugh and succeeds. Milo puts in the effort. It is for her that he sings like Tiny Tim, like Elvis, often switching between the two in a single song.

Milo wants to go to Riley. When Riley was a healthy dog they shared a special bond. They were both the jesters of the family. Riley could lie on his back, neck arched, head tilted seductively and legs spread-eagle. It was the "centerfold pose" that made Winona laugh, and even made his mother smile. This is the way the family seems to like Milo as well, in his ability to be ridiculous.

When Milo hears Winona enter the house and close the bathroom door he slips into her bedroom, kneels down in front of the dark mass that haunts the foot of the bed, and in the dim light tries to locate Riley's head. He wonders, did he really see Winona naked? Her body was so white and there were leaf patterns like lace over it, cast by the pool lights. Her head was thrown back at first, but when it came up it was not like her, it was more animal, she looked hungry, and then it seemed that every muscle on her face relaxed and her mouth fell open, and then she wasn't there at all.

Riley is not there either. There's no twitch to his nose, and the wrinkles of his forehead are slack. Riley's eyes are dull as scuffed black marbles; his hair is matted and clumped. Milo can't stand it. He wonders how Winona can bear to sleep with him. He wonders why his parents haven't just put him down. He picks Riley up and a thin burp, similar to the sound that came from the dog toy, slips out of Riley's mouth.

He takes Riley to the swimming pool. He wants to hold him under and feel him struggle. But he can't do that. And Riley might not struggle at all anyway, and that would be terrible too. He could drop him out of the tree house, but probably Riley would break all his bones and still not die. He could go get his father's gun from the garage. That would be the quickest and most manly thing to do—to shoot Riley in the head. Milo sits down to think about it. He crumples over Riley and cries.

9.

The next afternoon, after the family has gone to church, Norm retreats to the garage to putter around with his compressor and airbrush contraption. But he feels a little guilty. Church. Sitting together with his family in the pews makes him notice things. He noticed how Milo sat, not next to Winona, as usual, but next to him, slumped inward. He noticed how he didn't greet, smile, and talk to anyone who would listen. Norm was on the verge of thinking this a positive change when he started catching looks from Franny. In fact, he caught one as he stepped out the back door, headed to his sanctuary and his new project—a 1940 Ford convertible. So Norm hides his paints and new equipment, pats his car to reassure it, and hollers across the yard for Milo to come help him with the engine.

Inside the garage Milo stares listlessly under the old car's hood. Norm has instructed him to hold up a tube to funnel fluorescent-green coolant. After Norm pours the liquid he pats the flank of the car and jokes, "Let's tie up her tubes," signaling Milo to pull the tube out of the reservoir. Norm hopes this is a clever metaphor about controlling the fruits of a woman's sex drive. It's also a test for Milo—a joke that conveys knowledge of women's carnal power, for maybe Milo's slumping about a girl? But Milo doesn't seem to hear him. He runs his finger over a peeling decal on the inside of the car door—a mermaid with flowing hair and revealed breasts.

"What's this?" he asks.

"What?" says Norm.

"Aren't you going to take this sticker off?" Milo asks. He's really thinking it looks like a tattoo on shiny muscled skin.

Norm sighs.

"I think she's kind of cute," Norm says and winks.

"I guess you don't mind about Winona's, then," Milo says, surprised by the force of his voice. "I mean about her tattoo."

Norm doesn't immediately catch on. Milo, with his absurd performances, seldom tries to make sense, and Winona and tattoo don't go together. Winona is the best of Franny and himself. She's the one who gets things done, who is practical and will know how to make a living. She sits by him quietly and reads the morning paper. *Milo* is the one who does strange things to impress others. He's the one who sank his allowance into a pyramid scheme, who bought boxes of candy bars, not so he could make a profit, but so he could go door to door and get to know the neighbors.

Norm is irritated with Milo. Standing there looking at him, he's more irritated than usual with this son who is too big and friendly, and who is also, at least in these ways, too much like himself.

"Winona does not have a tattoo!" Norm yells. His voice backs Milo out the door.

Norm returns to the car, irritated, and confused at the force of his voice. But as he presses down the thought of the tattoo, an image of his mother pops up. His mother had one. Tiny, a heart on her shoulder blade. When he was little he thought it was there only for him because she called it her love button, and when he touched it she would turn around and give him a kiss.

His mother was beautiful then; she used hot rollers in a case that looked like an engine block, fluttery eyelashes stored in a box, and red lipstick put on with a fine brush, which made her lips look carved into her skin. But once Norm started high school she went out most nights, and that's mostly how he remembers her. His ideas of her exist in that time spent alone as a teenager, sitting at home waiting for his mom and thinking about girls. Once during this time, his mother brought a man home and he heard their muffled talk and music all night through his bedroom wall. And Norm saw his mother's breasts once, by accident, passing by her door when she didn't know he was home. She sat in front of her mirror, held them up, smiled, and ran her thumbs over her nipples.

Norm walks out into the yard where Winona is standing at an easel in long pants with her hair billowing around her head. Stuck, he looks at her for a long time. Until she turns around abruptly.

"Dad?" she says. He stands with his arms across his chest to level his look, to openly assess. He looks at her lips, which today carry a tinge of red, her hair, brushed out and full, her hips, her slight shoulders and fuller breasts. He looks at her in pieces.

"Your brother says you have a tattoo," he says. Winona puts her hands on the elastic band of her pants, to pull them down a notch, to show him. Norm yells, "Don't!" He turns on his heel and walks quickly back into the garage.

10.

Norm doesn't talk to Winona at the dinner table. He asks Milo to pass the butter, the salad, and the dressing, even though all these items sit in front of Winona, and Milo must stand and stretch his whole body across the table to deliver them. The first time his shirt smears along the butter. The second time he knocks over a decorative candlestick.

"Milo!" Franny scolds.

After dinner, when Winona sits down to watch TV, Norm gets up and leaves. Milo folds himself into the corner of the couch, looking at the television or his feet.

Franny knows there's something wrong. She watches Norm's change carefully. She's seen it before, this building up of pressure in his usually porous personality. She watches him with a feeling of dread and excitement, like the excitement over a novel's impending crises and fallout. She watches as if her chance is coming, as if the tables are about to turn. Franny watches Winona too, but doesn't dare approach. She knows Winona has begun to sense her neediness, her desire to be closer, although not like friends. She's seen where this type of mother-daughter relationship leads—to daughters who push, negotiate, and become publicly critical of their mothers.

It's a setup, this motherhood business, she thinks.

Franny puts the dishes away in the kitchen. They crash against each other. Usually, for Winona, this is the worst sound in the world. The brittle and tin clinks channel her mother's frustration and the endless drudgery of doing dishes in the first place—the fact that once they're all washed they'll be dirtied and need to be washed again.

But tonight she gets up to help, not out of guilt or a sense of duty, but to be close to her mother's body. She's felt a space open up around her mother lately, a space more like an unspoken need than an open invitation. This not being officially invited is the main reason she's avoided it and suffered her mother's small jabs in return. But now that her father is angry she needs her mom. Her dad has made her feel so full of something bad that she wouldn't mind dissolving a bit, into the water, into her mom's stiff and awkward welcome. She dips her hands in the hot water and her mother's movements slow down. Franny softens and can feel Winona's warmth. They stand this way, in the steam, until Norm enters the kitchen, at the usual time, for his fat-free pudding.

When Norm reaches into the refrigerator he feels warmth too, even though it's cold. He feels warmth from the refrigerator light and the fact of special food that is just for him. He's a child again, at his mother's house on shopping day, when once a month the refrigerator held two boxes of Moon Pies. He remembers the feeling of unwrapping the cellophane of the Moon Pie, and bringing it up to his mouth. It was always too intense, the pleasure too mixed with the knowledge of loss—knowing the boxes would last for two days and the rest of the food would only last two weeks. For the remaining two weeks they would eat out at the diner where his mother worked and sometimes negotiated free meals by flirting, if only a little, with the owner. As Norm closes the refrigerator door he notices the two women standing at the sink.

"Slut," he mumbles under his breath.

Franny gets confused. She's not sure to whom Norm is talking. She stops washing and looks at Winona who keeps working with rigid arms, scrubbing, scrubbing, straight posture, face carved in stone. She's a girl who will turn into a real taskmaster, a real bitch. Bitches and sluts, Franny thinks, the two great options. Why not give in, she thinks, why not embrace them both!

Franny moves toward Norm, raises her hand, and slaps him so hard his head jerks to the side and his pudding tumbles to the floor.

Winona turns in time to see her mother's hand hit. She hears it crack across the kitchen like the opening of thunder, and it changes her inside—it evaporates some of the shame that's been accumulating from her father's look, some of the feeling that's been welling and surging, tempting to come pouring out of her eyes. And the slap happens so fast that "slut" doesn't have a chance to travel across the room and attach itself to her—it hovers midair. It retreats back to her father, so she hears the teenage boy in him, the lust and the hurt that's required to say this word in that way, the low grumble of it.

Her mother has become her hero.

But Milo, standing in the kitchen doorway, sees the slap too, and feels as if it were for him. It's his fault he had the erection. He was spying when he saw Winona naked. He told her secret to his dad.

Milo runs to find Riley for comfort as he usually does. In fact, the whole family looks to Riley for comfort when they sit awkward and wordless at the dinner table. They look to the dog. And Riley will drool and cock his head in glee at the mention of his name, assuming every act of attention an act of love. Milo gathers Riley in his arms and carries him into the kitchen. He sets him, a mangled centerpiece, on the lazy Susan where he rotates slowly between the two candlesticks.

They look at him expectantly: Winona, Franny, Milo, and Norm. They wait for him to roll over, spread his legs, wiggle. Instead, Riley lies there motionless, bouncing the family's stillness back out to them.

"He's dead!" Milo yells angrily, as if it's his mother's, his father's, Winona's fault.

And Norm believes him.

"Oh," Norm says, in a moan that they all feel in their stomachs. It's a moan that causes Franny to believe he's dead as well, to put her hand over her mouth and tremble, and to remember her mother, hooked up to tubes in the nursing home. Her mother, whom she must visit.

Winona feels her father's moan but knows that Riley died a long time ago, knows that what is sitting on the kitchen table is just a living emptiness, a container.

She looks at Riley. She observes him intently, focuses down to his molecules. He's where everything that should exist gets sucked down. He's where her father says, "I'm sorry," understands the anger in her mother's slap, and has not yet looked at her in that terrible way—in pieces. Riley is where Milo gets a girlfriend. He is where Winona is now turning and touching her mother's skin. He is where there's a trickle of water from Franny, a light spurting, a gush, and then a flood. Franny is squeezing Winona so tightly that Winona sees it must really be happening.

Franny says, "I'm sorry, I'm sorry about Riley"—she is folding her, cinching her in. Riley is where Winona is beginning to see that it's her mother she is bound to, even though it feels as if Franny is breaking Winona's bones.

Credits

Some of these stories have appeared or are forthcoming in *The Literary Review Web*, *The Northwestern Review*, *The Mississippi Review*, *Connu*, *Prompt*, *DIAGRAM*, and *The Iowa Review*.

Book Club Guide

1. The endings of several stories in *Elegies for Uncanny Girls* rest on slight shifts in the narrators' perspectives. In "Other Mothers" the narrator sees a woman in a café as alternately a French feminist, an overwhelmed mother, and finally something in between those extremes. What is the effect of these shifts in perspective? Do they make the narrator less reliable? More real? How did you experience them?

2. "Center" is another story in which the resolution rests on a grounding of the narrator's perspective. By the end of the story Susan is able to "come out of memory" into the present moment with her brother. What role does memory play in the story? Do you think Susan's memories are entirely reliable? How might Susan's return to memories help or hinder her ability to find peace in her relationship with her brother and mother?

3. Mothers play a large role in this collection. How would you characterize some of the mother-daughter relationships in it?

4. In "Costume," "Center," and "Audra" mothers are positioned by the young narrators as subtle adversaries. In "Costume," when Meredith insists on designing her own Halloween costume, she feels her mother regard her as suspicious, "slippery, like a piece of unstitchable satin." In "Center" Susan feels that her mother gives her brother more encouragement for his efforts. And in

"Audra" Molly feels confined by her mother's platitudes about good behavior.

On the other hand, the mothers are simply acting in line with cultural dictates—they are protecting, molding, and instilling values. In what way might these mothers, or mothers in general, serve as scapegoats for larger cultural problems regarding gender roles?

In "Winona," Franny characterizes motherhood as a setup. Why do you think Franny feels this way? What about American culture may set mothers up to feel trapped, lonely, or like failures?

5. The voices of mothers are only heard at the beginning and the end of this collection. First is the young bewildered mother of "Other Mothers." At the end is the jaded Franny, of "Winona." What is the effect of bracketing the collection in this way?

6. Some of the stories in *Elegies* show the narrators in the act of storytelling. In "Details" and "When Maggie Thinks of Matt" we get to witness both narrators piecing narratives together, gathering details, dismissing certain experiences as unwritable. In the case of "Details," the narrator gets to the end of her story and decides to start over with a new beginning. Does this discount what she's already told us? What might this story tell us about our desire or need to tell stories? What role do stories play in our lives?

7. In "When Maggie Thinks of Matt," the narrator constructs an elegy or remembrance of her relationship with Matt. At different points she tells us that she's writing down what she would have wanted him to be thinking or saying, or what she would have liked to have said herself. How does this avowal strike you? Does it add anything to the emotional impact of the story? Have you ever found yourself narrating your own experiences in this way?

8. Many of the stories suspend narrative, or plot, to capture moments, or to carefully distill an experience. "Caroline" starts with a memory of a childhood game under pomegranate trees, and threads many other lyrical moments through the action of the story. How do you experience the lyrical moments in "Caroline," or in other stories? What do the lyrical moments do for the stories that more traditional narration can't do? How might the lyrical moments serve the purpose of elegizing?

9. A few of these stories deal with friendships between girls. How are the friendships in "Audra" and "Caroline" different? In both stories the girls experience their identities as deeply tied to their relationships with friends. The narrator of "Caroline" wants to blend into Caroline. Why? As a way to erase the differences in their bodies? To deny the onset of puberty, or entry into a world where male and female are established hierarchical categories?

In "Audra," a ghostly girl is a welcome wedge in a friendship that Molly feels is based on her inferiority and Cindy's superiority. Is this kind of interdependence of identity a staple of female friendship, or is it characteristic of other kinds of relationships as well?

"When Maggie Thinks of Matt" may also be read as a story of female friendship, though Matt is nominally and physically a man. How is Maggie and Matt's relationship similar to some of the female friendships in the collection?

10. The narrator in "Caroline" is writing a memory of a personal experience, and the narrator of "Audra" speaks from a third-person perspective, which sometimes dips into the future tense. How would you describe the effect of these different narrative styles? What do the different authorial perspectives allow, or open up, within the emotional body of each story?

11. Freud described the experience of the uncanny as a series of three or more appearances of seemingly linked odd, unreal, or unfamiliar phenomena—as a kind of multiple déjà vu that fills us with foreboding or unease. In *Elegies for Uncanny Girls*, Audra appears five times. The narrator of "Other Mothers" is haunted by the repeated appearance of vulnerable babies. What other stories capture this sense of the uncanny? Did you notice other uncanny "pop-up" images or phenomena throughout the collection? In what ways do the girls and women in the book experience themselves, or their bodies, as odd, unreal, or unfamiliar?

12. Many of the stories create large interior landscapes for their characters to dwell and dream inside. Some characters, such as Winona, are very at home in these landscapes, while some, such as Susan in "Center," feel trapped or hindered by their inner dialogues. How do you experience the characters' interiority? Do these spaces of interior narration feel isolating, claustrophobic, enriching, revelatory? How do these moments function in relation to the more external moments of dialogue and action? How does the interiority function in relation to the unreal elements in the stories, such as a mother's split wrists, Dora's partial invisibility, and the big little lady's shifts in size? Does the interiority help the surreal moments feel real?

JENNIFER COLVILLE is the founding editor of *PromptPress*, a journal for visual art inspired by writing and writing inspired by visual art. Jennifer holds an MFA from Syracuse University and a PhD in English and creative writing from the University of Utah. She lives in Iowa City with her husband and two children.

CPSIA information can be obtained
at www.ICGtesting.com
Printed in the USA
BVOW08s1213200117
474047BV00001B/6/P